THE 104-STOREY TREEHOUSE

Andy Griffiths lives in a 104-storey treehouse with his friend Terry and together they make funny books, just like the one you're holding in your hands right now. Andy writes the words and Terry draws the pictures. If you'd like to know more, read this book (or visit www.andygriffiths.com.au).

Terry Denton lives in a 104-storey treehouse with his friend Andy and together they make funny books, just like the one you're holding in your hands right now. Terry draws the pictures and Andy writes the words. If you'd like to know more, read this book (or visit www.terrydenton.com).

*Climb higher every time
with the Treehouse series*

ANDY GRIFFITHS

THE 104-STOREY TREEHOUSE

BY
ANDY GRIFFITHS
& TERRY DENTON

MACMILLAN CHILDREN'S BOOKS

First published 2018 in Pan by Pan Macmillan Australia Pty Limited

First published in the UK 2018 by Macmillan Children's Books
an imprint of Pan Macmillan
20 New Wharf Road, London N1 9RR
Associated companies throughout the world
www.panmacmillan.com

ISBN 978-1-5098-3377-1

Text copyright © Flying Beetroot Pty Ltd 2018
Illustrations copyright © Terry Denton 2018

The right of Andy Griffiths and Terry Denton to be identified as the
author and illustrator of this work has been asserted by them in
accordance with the Copyright, Designs and Patents Act 1988.

5 7 9 8 6 4

A CIP catalogue record for this book is available from the British Library.

Typeset in 14/18 Minion Pro by Seymour Designs
Printed and bound by CPI Group (UK) Ltd, Croydon CR0 4YY

CONTENTS

Who am I?

CHAPTER 1

THE 104-STOREY TREEHOUSE

Hi, my name is Andy (*moan*).

A Andy (I just told you that!).

This is my friend Terry (*groan*).

Q What did the rock say when it rolled into the tree?

We live in a tree (*moan, groan*).

A   Nothing—rocks don't talk.

Well, when I say 'tree', I mean treehouse.
And when I say 'treehouse', I don't just mean any old treehouse—I mean a 104-*storey* treehouse!
(It used to be a 91-storey treehouse, but we've added another 13 storeys.)

This is not an official new level! (The goats are just being annoying!)

Q Which side of a tree has the most leaves?

So what are you waiting for?
Come on up!

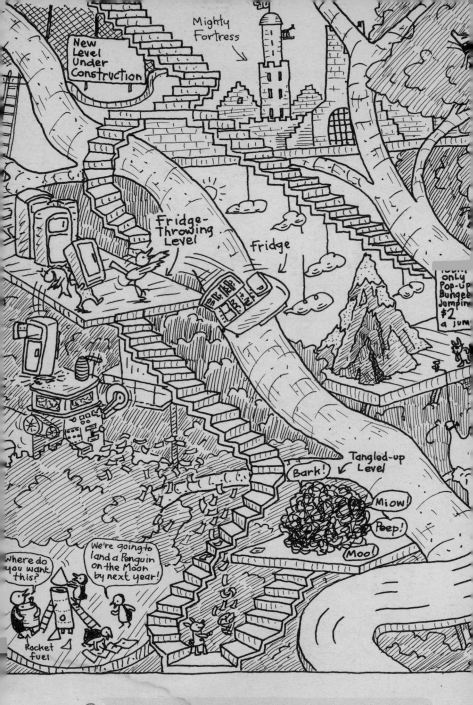

Q How did the idiot get hurt raking leaves?

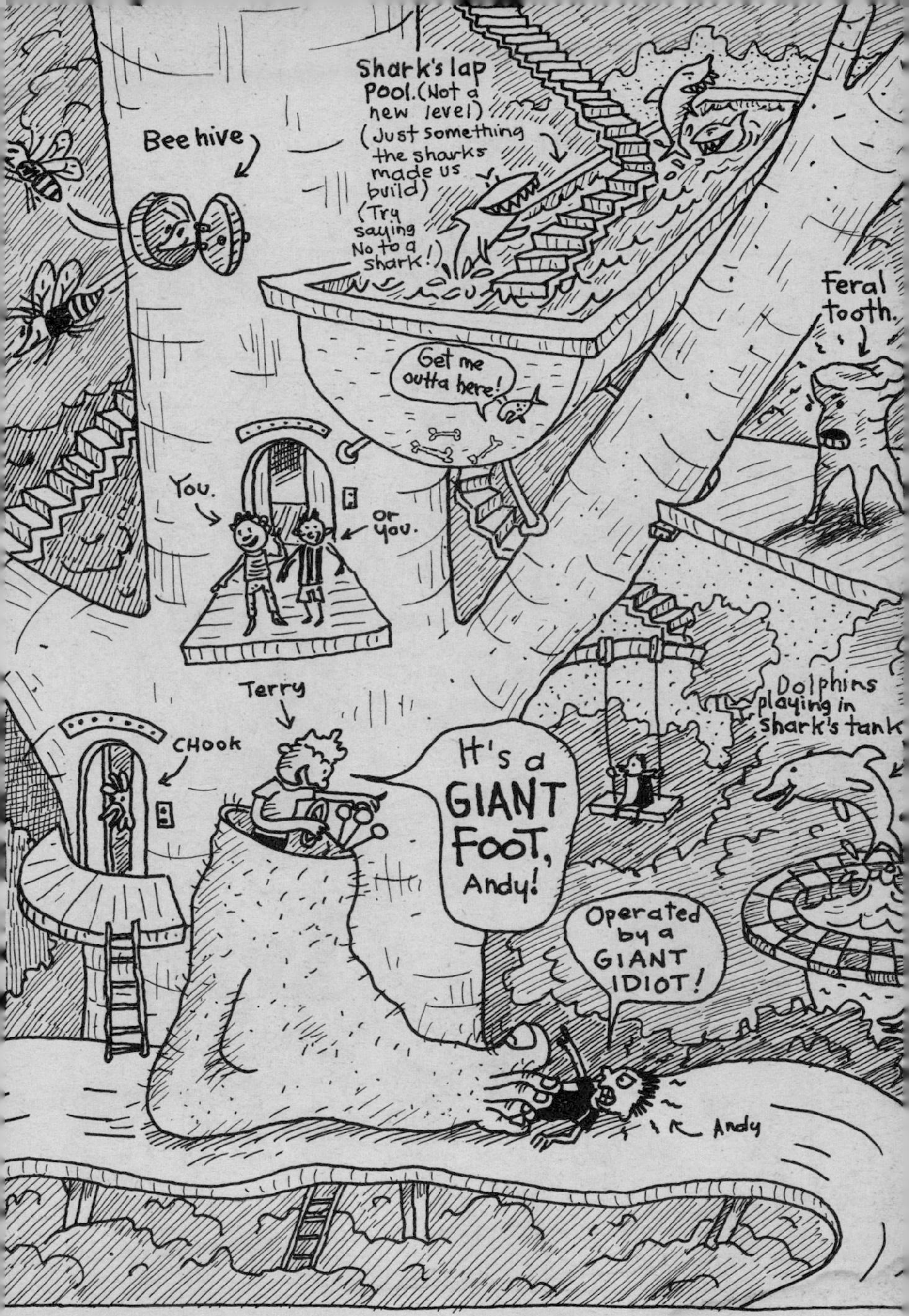
Shark's lap pool. (Not a new level) (Just something the sharks made us build) (Try saying No to a shark!)
Bee hive
Feral tooth.
Get me outta here!
You.
or you.
Terry
CHOOK
It's a GIANT FOOT, Andy!
Dolphins playing in shark's tank
Operated by a GIANT IDIOT!
Andy

A He fell out of the tree.

It's got a stupid-hat level,

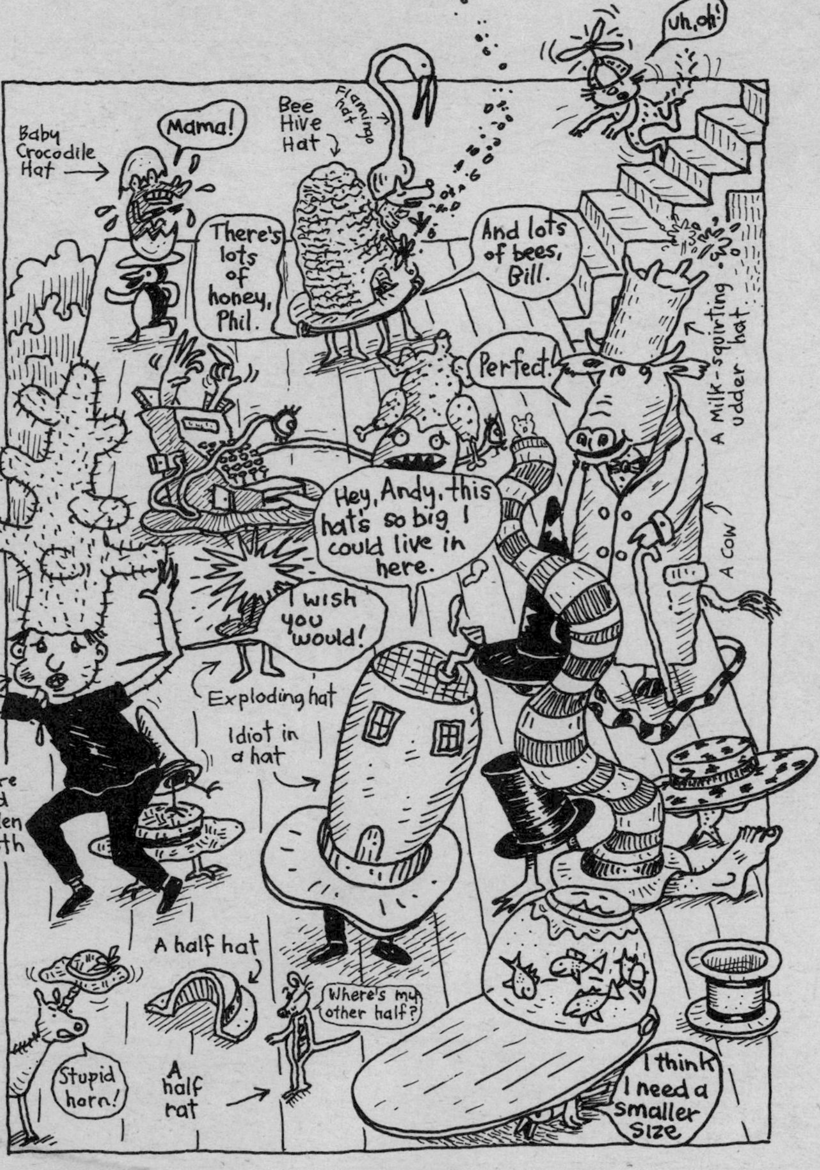
Uh, oh!
Baby Crocodile Hat
Mama!
Bee Hive Hat
Flamingo hat
There's lots of honey, Phil.
And lots of bees, Bill.
Annoying Cactus Hat
Perfect.
A Milk-squirting udder hat
Hey, Andy, this hat's so big I could live in here.
A cow
Prickles
I wish you would!
Exploding hat
Idiot in a hat
Sore and swollen tooth
A half hat
Where's my other half?
Stupid horn!
A half rat
I think I need a smaller size

 Q Where does Dracula keep his money?

a money-making machine (that also makes honey),

a never-ending staircase,

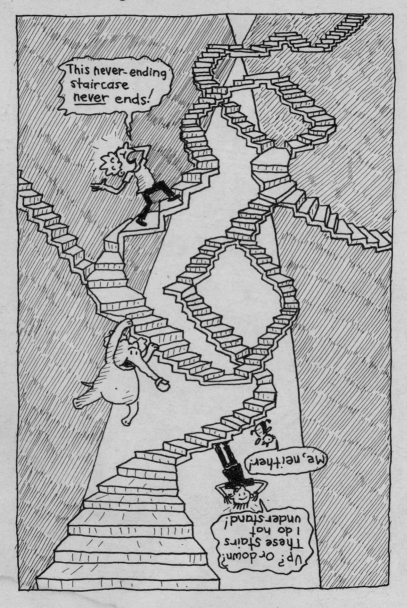

Q   How do shells get around in the ocean?

a Two-Dollar Shop (there's nothing *over* two dollars),

a Two-Million-Dollar Shop (there's nothing *under* two million dollars),

Q Why did the boy fall off his bike?

a refrigerator-throwing range (with a refrigerator-vending machine so we never run out of refrigerators),

A Because his mother threw a fridge at him.

a bunfighting level (with a bun-vending machine
so we never run out of buns),

Q   How can you say 'rabbit' without using the letter R?

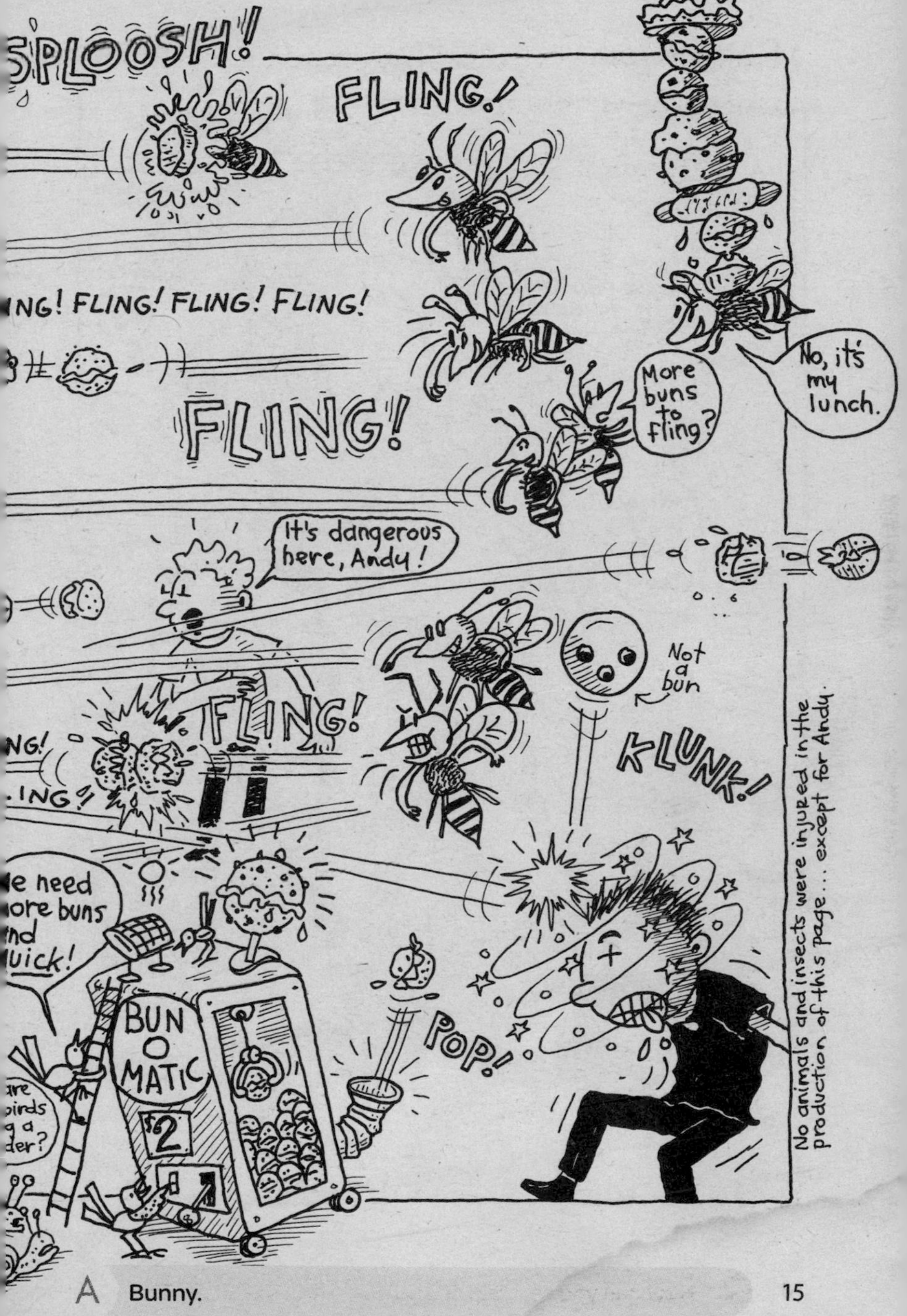
SPLOOSH!
FLING!
NG! FLING! FLING! FLING!
FLING!
More buns to fling?
No, it's my lunch.
It's dangerous here, Andy!
Not a bun
FLING!
NG!
ING!
KLUNK!
e need
ore buns
nd
uick!
BUN O MATIC
$2
POP!
No animals and insects were injured in the production of this page... except for Andy.

Mount Everest,

Q What was the tallest mountain in the world before Mount Everest was discovered?

a burp bank,

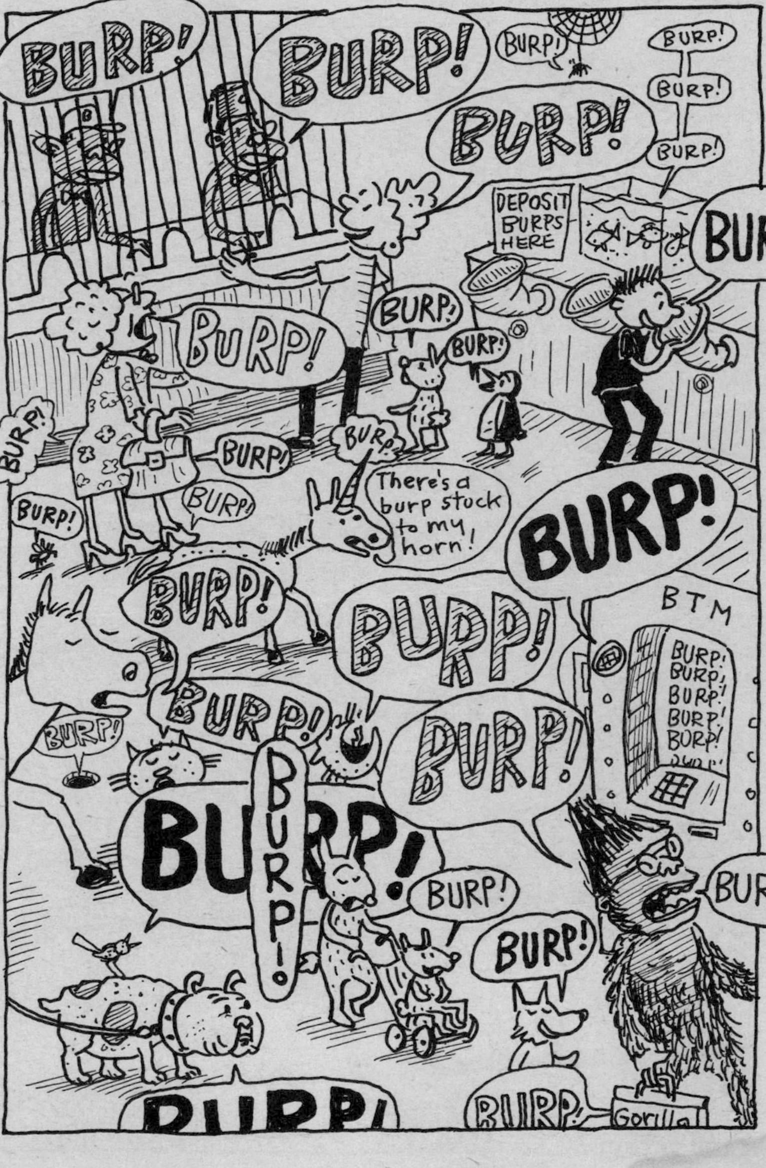
BURP!
BURP!
BURP!
BURP!
BURP!
BURP!
BURP!
DEPOSIT BURPS HERE
BURP!
BURP!
BURP!
BURP!
BURP!
BURP!
BURP!
BURP!
BURP!
There's a burp stuck to my horn!
BURP!
BTM
BURP!
BURP!
BURP!
BURP!
BURP!
BURP!
BURP!
BURP!
BURP!
BURP!
BURP!
BURP!
BURP!
BURP!
BURP!
Gorilla

a tangled-up level (where everything is really, REALLY tangled up),

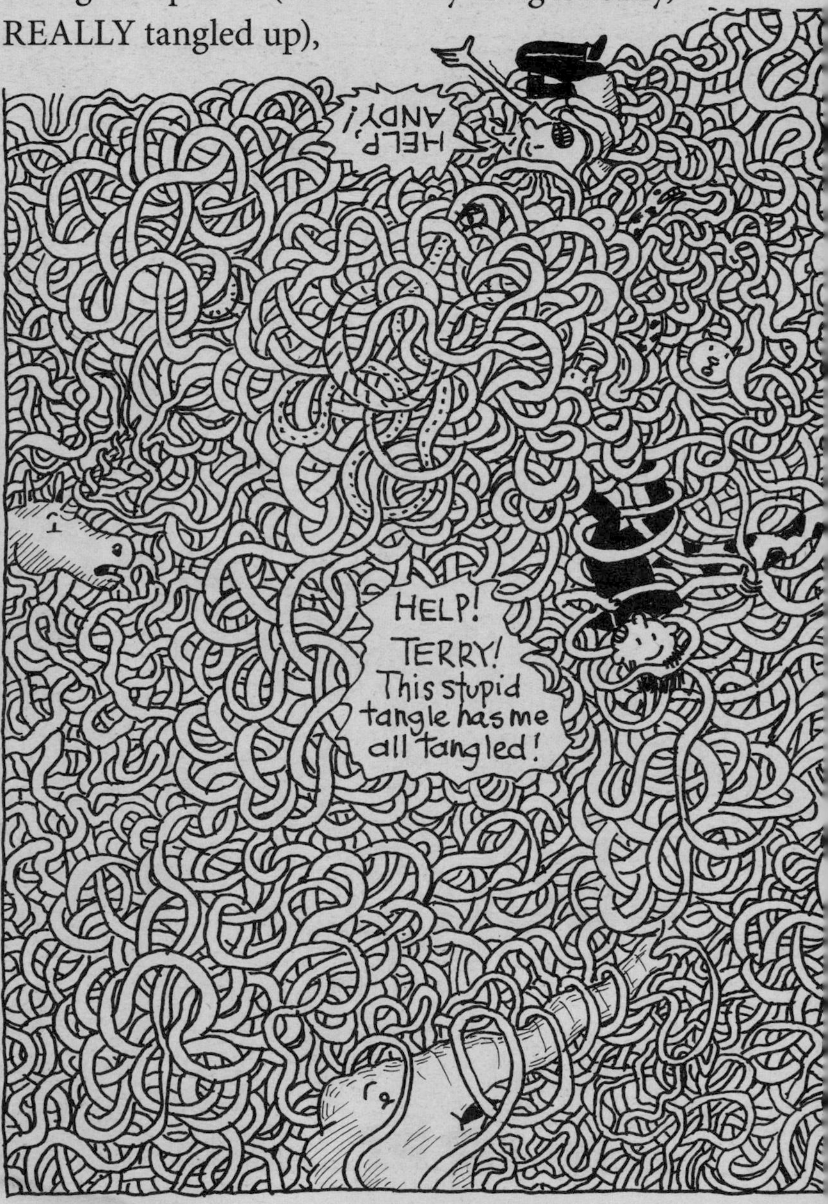
HELP, ANDY!
HELP! TERRY! This stupid tangle has me all tangled!

Q What do snakes do after a fight?

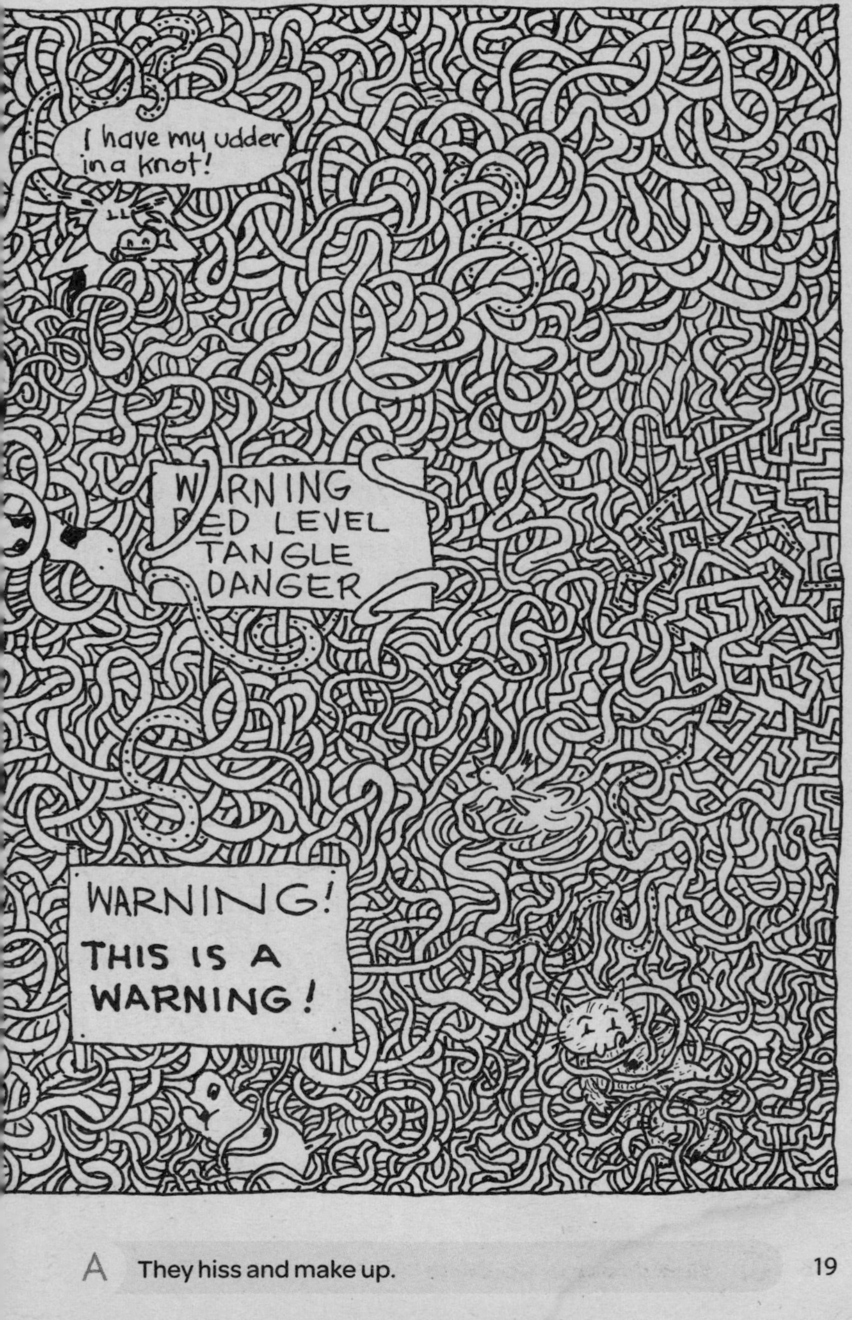
I have my udder in a knot!
WARNING
RED LEVEL
TANGLE
DANGER
WARNING!
THIS IS A
WARNING!

a deep-thoughts thinking room,

Q   What is pink and can think?

a mighty fortress reinforced with extra-strong
fortress reinforcer,

and a beautiful sunny meadow full of buttercups, butterflies and bluebirds.

Blue

Q Where do butterflies sleep?

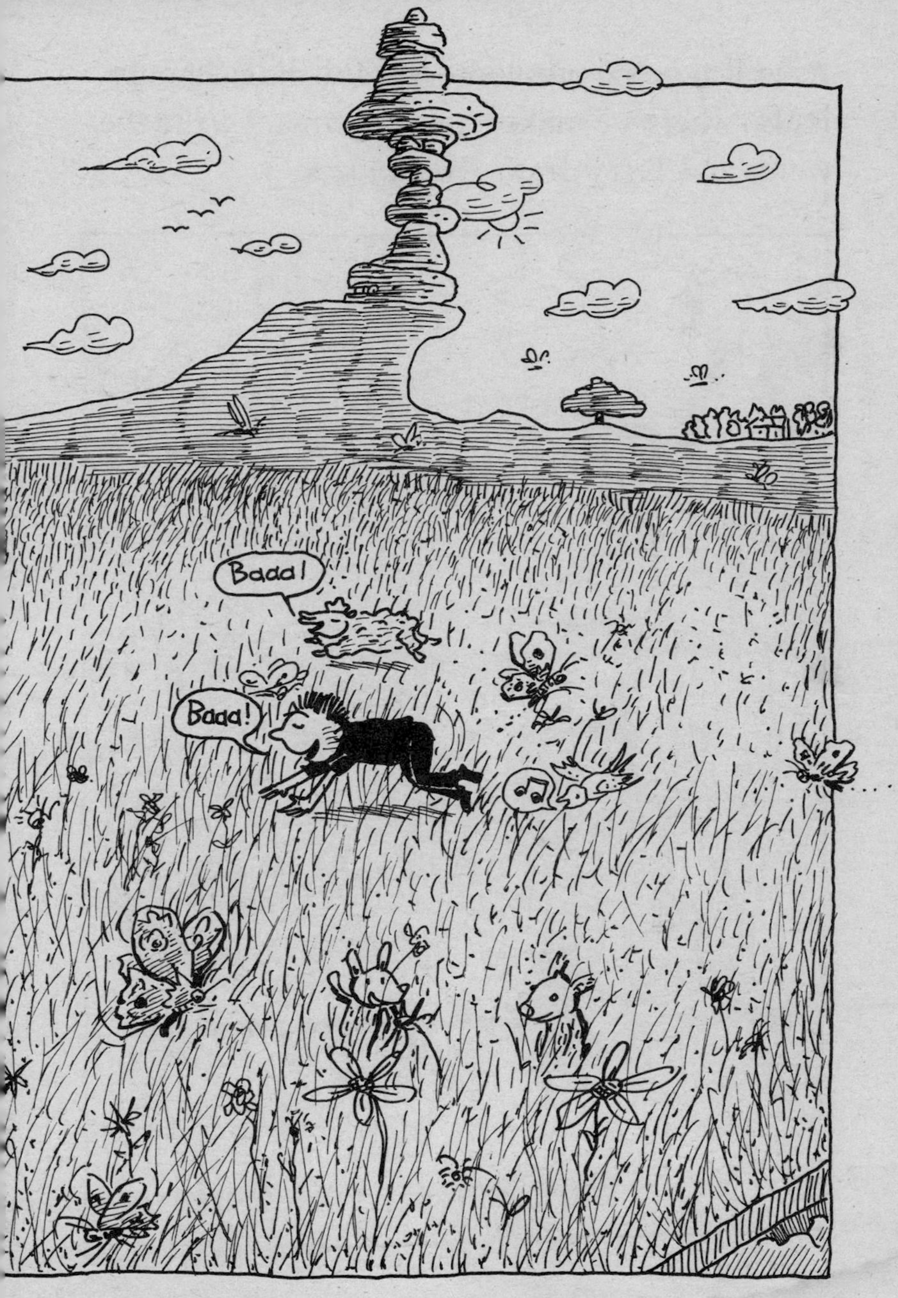
Baaa!
Baaa!

A On cater-pillows.

As well as being our home (*moan*), the treehouse is also where we make books together. I write the words and Terry draws the pictures.

Why did the fly fall off the wall?

As you can see (*groan*), we've been doing this for quite a while now.

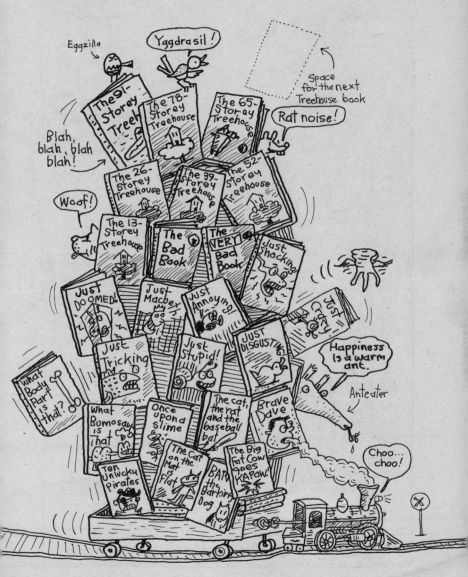

There are, of course, a lot of distractions in a 104-storey treehouse (*moan*) …

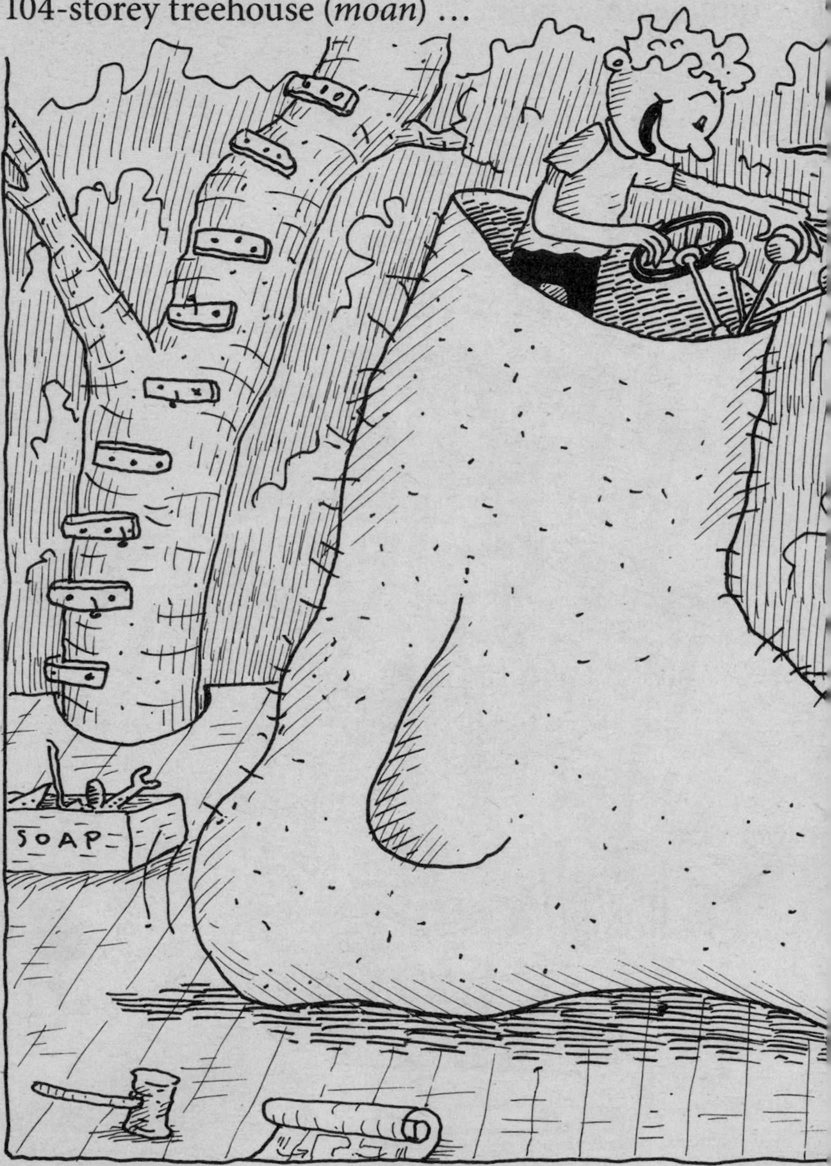
SOAP

Q What's grey?

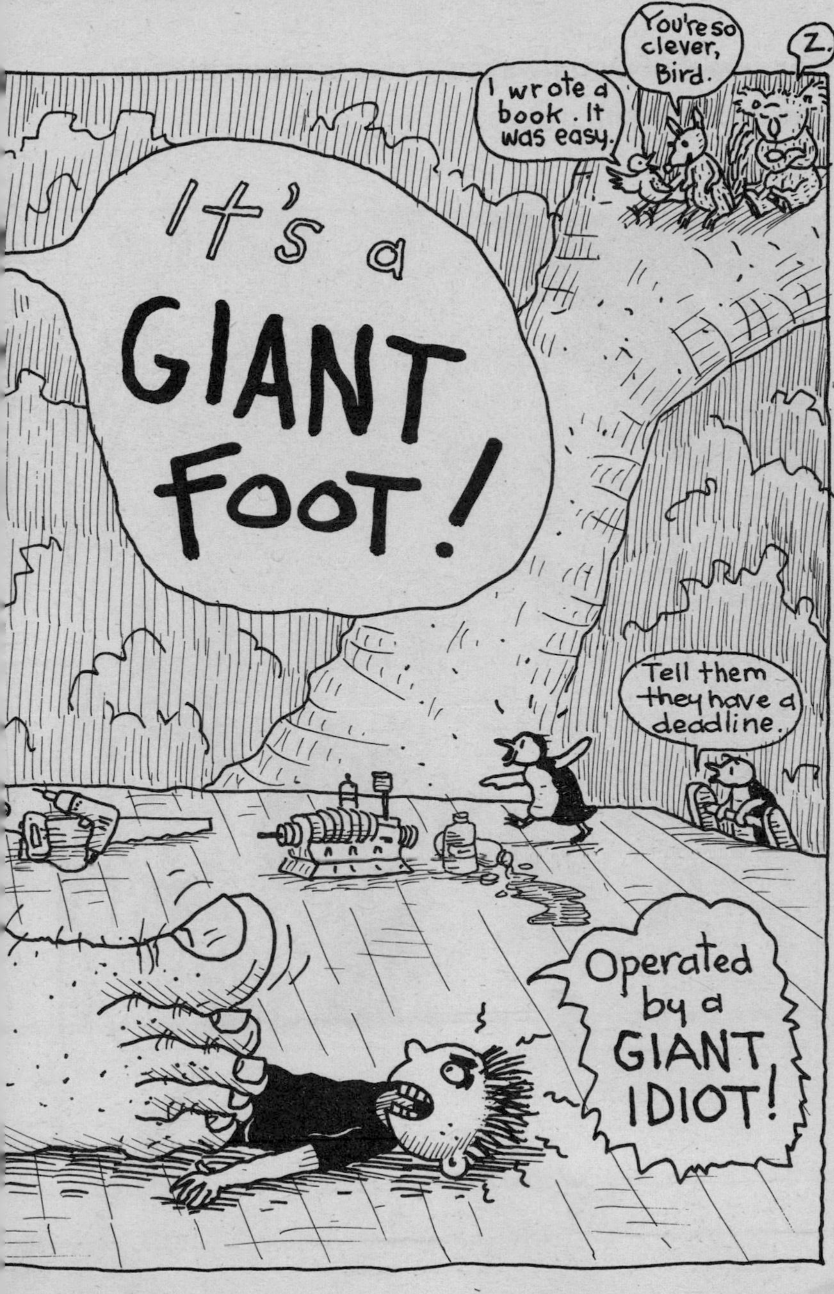

I wrote a book. It was easy.
You're so clever, Bird.
Z.
It's a GIANT FOOT!
Tell them they have a deadline.
Operated by a GIANT IDIOT!

A A melted penguin.

but somehow we always get our book written in the end (*groan*).

Q Why did the boy throw his clock out the window?

CHAPTER 2

ANDY'S ACHING TOOTHACHE

If you're like most of our readers (*moan*), you're probably wondering (*groan*) why I'm moaning and groaning so much. Well, the reason is I've got a really bad toothache.

'Hi, Andy,' says Terry, prancing towards me with a couple of lambs by his side. 'What a lovely day it is in our beautiful sunny meadow full of buttercups, butterflies and bluebirds!'

'No, it's not,' I say. 'It's a terrible day! I've got the most aching toothache in the world!'

'Hey, that reminds me of a joke,' says Terry. 'What time did the boy go to the dentist?'

'I don't know and I don't care!' I say. 'My tooth is hurting!'

'That's right,' he says, laughing. 'Two-thirty. Get it? Tooth-hurty. Just like you!'

'Yes, I get it,' I say.

'Then why aren't you laughing?'

'Because my tooth is hurting too much! It's hard to laugh when I'm in so much pain.'

'That's too bad,' says Terry, 'because I love jokes! I reckon we should write a whole book of them.'

'I'd love to,' I say, 'but with this toothache I just don't feel funny enough to write jokes. In fact, I'm not sure I even feel funny enough to write *this* book.'

Q If life gets tough, what do you have that you can always count on?

'But we *have* to write this book,' says Terry. 'Otherwise, Mr Big Nose will get mad!'

'I *know*,' I say. 'I just don't know how we're going to do it. This toothache is killing me.'

'Hey, look up there in the sky!' says Terry. 'It's a bird!'

I look up to where Terry's pointing. 'I don't think it's a bird,' I say. 'That's Superfinger.'

'No, it's not a bird *or* Superfinger,' says Terry. 'It's a *biplane*! And it's got a sign!'

Q Why did the plane crash?

TODAY

FUNNY EVEN WHEN YOU DON'T

NECDOTES, RIDDLES, RHYMES, ETC.

'A joke-writing pencil, Andy!' says Terry. 'That's exactly what *we* need! It could help us write jokes and it might even help us write our book even though you have a toothache. We should get one. Today!'

'But where from?' I say, just as a second biplane flies overhead.

'From a Two-Dollar Shop, that's where!' says Terry. 'And we've got a Two-Dollar Shop right here in our treehouse!'

'You're right,' I say (*moan*). 'But I've only got one dollar.'

'Darn, I've only got one dollar as well,' says Terry.
'Hmmm …' I say.

'Hmmm ...'

'Hmmm ...'

'Hmmm ...'

'Hmmm ...'

Q What did one maths book say to the other maths book?

'I've got an idea!'
says Terry. 'Why don't
we put our two one-
dollar coins together
and then we'll have
two dollars?!'

'Would that even
work?' I say. 'Is it even
possible? Do the laws
of mathematics even
allow such a thing?'

'I think they do,'
says Terry. 'But
there's only one way
to find out for sure.
Let's go to the
Two-Dollar Shop
and see if Pinchy
McPhee will let us
buy a two-dollar Joke
Writer 2000™ with our
two one-dollar coins!'

'I didn't know our sunny meadow had a video phone,' says Terry.

'Of course it does,' I say. 'Most meadows do these days.'

'I hope it's not Mr Big Nose,' says Terry.
'I'm afraid it might be,' I say.
'I'm afraid, too,' says Terry.

Q What demands an answer but asks no question?

I answer the phone. 'Hello (*moan*), Mr Big Nose,'
I groan.

'What's with all the moaning and groaning?!'
shouts Mr Big Nose, scaring a flock of butterflies
fluttering close to the screen. 'I don't have time to
listen to moaning and groaning! I'm a busy man,
you know!'

'I know,' I say, 'but my tooth—'

'I don't have time for explanations,' interrupts
Mr Big Nose. 'And neither do you. Your book is
due today. It had better be on my desk by two-thirty,
or else!'

'Well, we're running a bit behind,' I say, 'because of my toothache, but we've got a good idea to put lots of jokes in—'

Mr Big Nose interrupts me again. 'How about this for a joke?' he says. 'What's big and red and gets bigger and redder the angrier it gets and then explodes if a certain writer and illustrator don't get their book to me by the deadline, which, just in case you've forgotten, is 2.30 p.m. today?'

Q What's big and red and eats rocks?

'Um, beats me,' says Terry.

'Me too,' I say. 'We give up.'

'MY NOSE!' shouts Mr Big Nose. 'THAT'S WHAT! SO YOU'D BETTER GET IT DONE BY TWO-THIRTY TODAY, OR ELSE!'

A   A big red rock-eater.

'Yes, Mr Big Nose,' I say, but he's already gone.

'I didn't think that was a very funny joke,' says Terry.
'No, I think it was more of a *threat* than a joke,' I say. 'We'd better get to the Two-Dollar Shop and buy a Joke Writer 2000™ fast!'

'Let's take our jet-propelled swivel chairs,' says
Terry. 'It's quite a long way up.'

Terry whistles and the chairs appear instantly.

We jump on.

'To the Two-Dollar Shop!' yells Terry, as we take off at jet-propelled, supersonic swivel chair speed.

Q   What rocks but does not roll?

CHAPTER 3

PENS, PENCILS AND WRITING UTENSILS

We arrive at the Two-Dollar Shop. Pinchy McPhee is out the front, waving his claws around and singing at the top of his voice.

A A rocking chair.

Grand Sale! Grand Sale!
I'm having a great grand sale!
All items in my Two-Dollar Shop
Are priced at just TWO DOLLARS a pop!

Not one, not three
Not five: just TWO!
Just TWO dollars!
It's amazing—but true!

So—

'Excuse me, Pinchy,' I say quickly (before he can start a third verse), 'but isn't everything in the Two-Dollar Shop *always* only two dollars?'

'Of course,' says Pinchy. 'But today is a *grand sale* so two dollars is an extra-special price!'

Terry frowns. 'But if everything is *normally* two dollars and your *sale* price is two dollars, how is today different from any other day?'

'Because any other day is *not* a grand sale and today *is*!' says Pinchy, getting slightly crabby and waving his claws dangerously close to us.

We nod and step into the shop before he can get any crabbier.

'Wow!' says Terry. 'This shop has everything! Check it out!'

SMALL RIVER $2

$2

50 Q What do you call a sheep without legs?

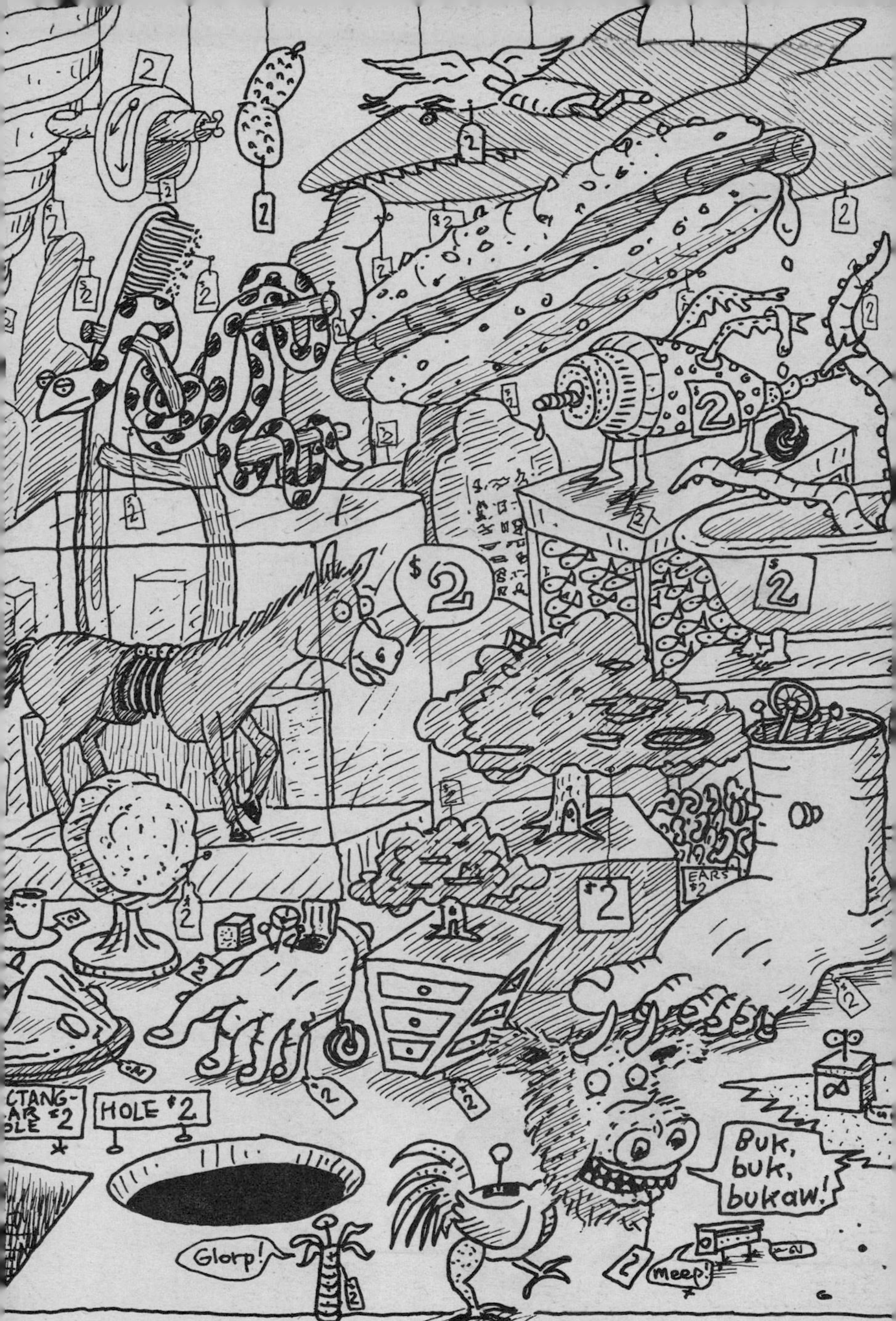
$2
HOLE $2
EARS $2
Buk, buk, bukaw!
Glorp!
meep!

A A cloud.

'Hey, look at this electric banana,' says Terry. 'It's only *two* dollars!'

'And this giant glow-in-the-dark marshmallow is bigger than my *head*,' he says. 'And it's only two dollars, too!'

Q What's yellow and smells like bananas?

'And check out this model of our treehouse!' says Terry. 'We could buy it and have a treehouse in our treehouse!'

'And there's also a model of the model of the treehouse!' he says. 'We could have a treehouse in our treehouse in our treehouse!'

'Oh, wow!' says Terry, picking up a golden toilet seat. 'Here's that solid gold toilet seat we've always wanted—and it's only two dollars as well! Can we get it, Andy? Please, please, please, please, please, please? A solid gold toilet seat would solve *all* our problems!'

'No, it wouldn't,' I say. 'We came to buy a Joke Writer 2000™ and that's what we're going to do. *That* is going to solve all our problems.'

'Oh, yeah, I forgot,' says Terry, turning to Pinchy. 'Excuse me, Pinchy, do you sell pencils?'

'Of course I do,' says Pinchy. He takes a deep breath and starts singing.

♪ I have pens and pencils and writing utensils
Of all sorts right here in my store:
I have dip pens and gel pens and ballpoints
   and biros
And textas and markers galore! ♪

I have a pen you can use as a lipstick,
And a pen that can write under water,
And a pen for writing excuses,
In case you haven't done something you oughta.

I have a pen that can write upside down
Like the astronauts took into space,
And a pen you can use to write notes on your hand.
Or-if you prefer-on your face.

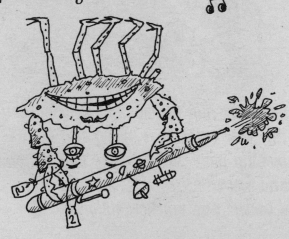

Q Where do astronauts park their spaceships?

And here is a pen,
My pen-loving friends,
That comes with a little night-light.
You can write in the night
For as long as you like
Because the little night-light is quite bright!

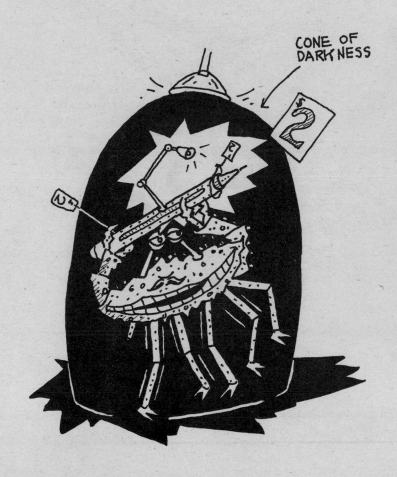

CONE OF DARKNESS

A **Parking meteors.**

And here is a pen
With a fan on the end—
You can use it to write when it's hot.
And it also comes with a heater attached
So you can write whether it's hot or it's not.

crab legs

It also converts to a helicopter... and all for a mere $2

Q   What did one pencil say to the other pencil?

I have a pen that writes with invisible ink,
That's particularly good for spies,
And a pen that always tells the truth
And one that will only write lies.

I have a pen that changes into a car,
And one that turns into a jet.
And a pen with fur and ears and a tail—
It's the next best thing to a pet!

So, as you can see, I have all you could need,
And no pen is priced over two dollars.
I have bargains galore in my two-dollar store
For authors, illustrators and scholars!

'So, what will it be?' says Pinchy. 'What type of pen or pencil would you like?'

'A Joke Writer 2000™, please,' I say.

'I'm afraid I'm clean out of them,' says Pinchy. 'They've been very popular this morning, thanks to my biplane advertising campaign. But, not to worry, I have lots of other wonderful pens and pencils.'

He takes a deep breath.

'Uh-oh,' whispers Terry. 'I think he's going to sing again.'

'No, it's okay, Pinchy,' I say quickly. 'We really just want a Joke Writer 2000™.'

'I guess you could try Fancy Fish's Two-Million-Dollar Shop,' says Pinchy. 'He might have one.'

'Thanks, Pinchy!' says Terry. 'We'll go there right now.'

We fly to the Two-Million-Dollar Shop as fast as we can without stopping.

The Two-Million-Dollar Shop is much better than the Two-Dollar Shop, but, of course, all the stuff is a lot more expensive.

'Wow!' says Terry. 'This shop has everything! Check it out!'

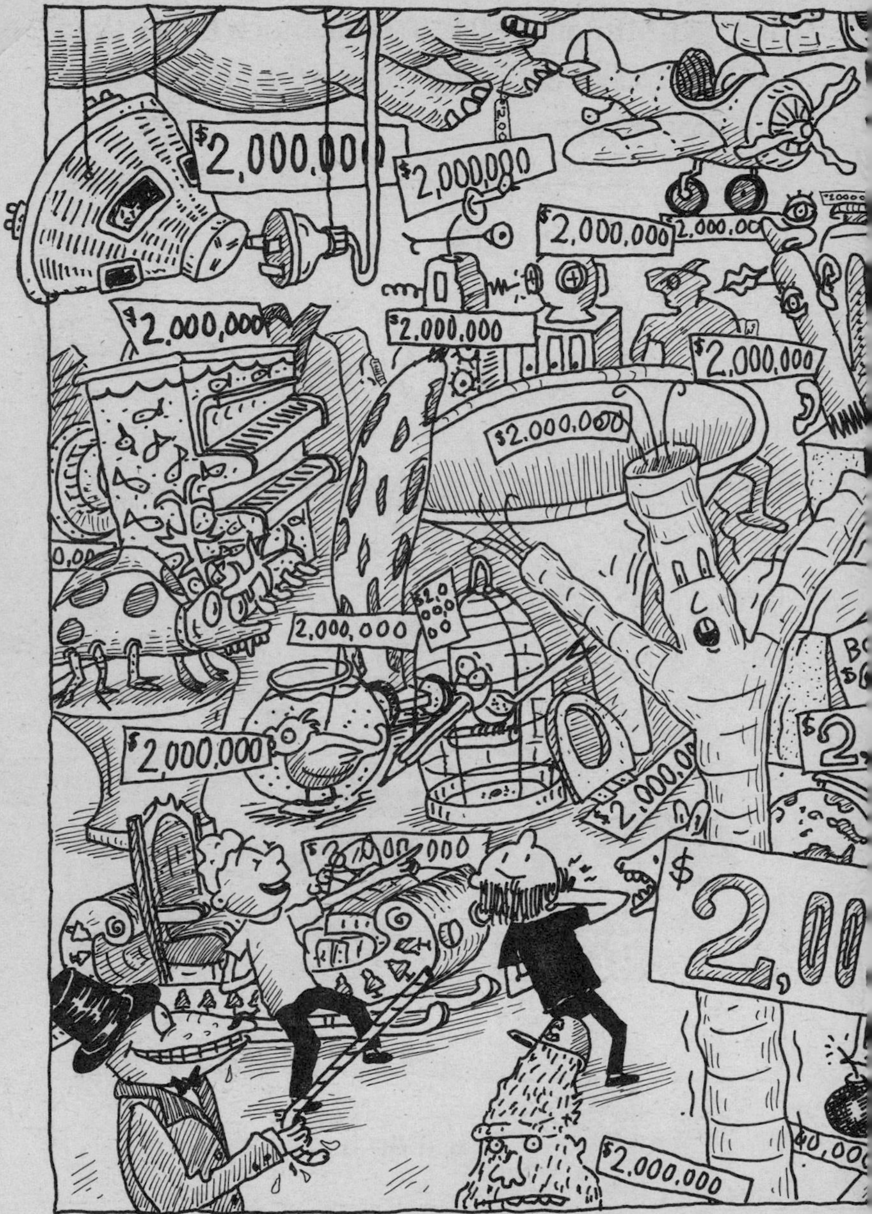
$2,000,000
$2,000,000
$2,000,000
2,000,00
$2,000,000
$2,000,000
$2,000,000
$2,000,000
2,000,000
$2,000,000
$2,000,000
$2,000,000

 Q Why do birds fly south?

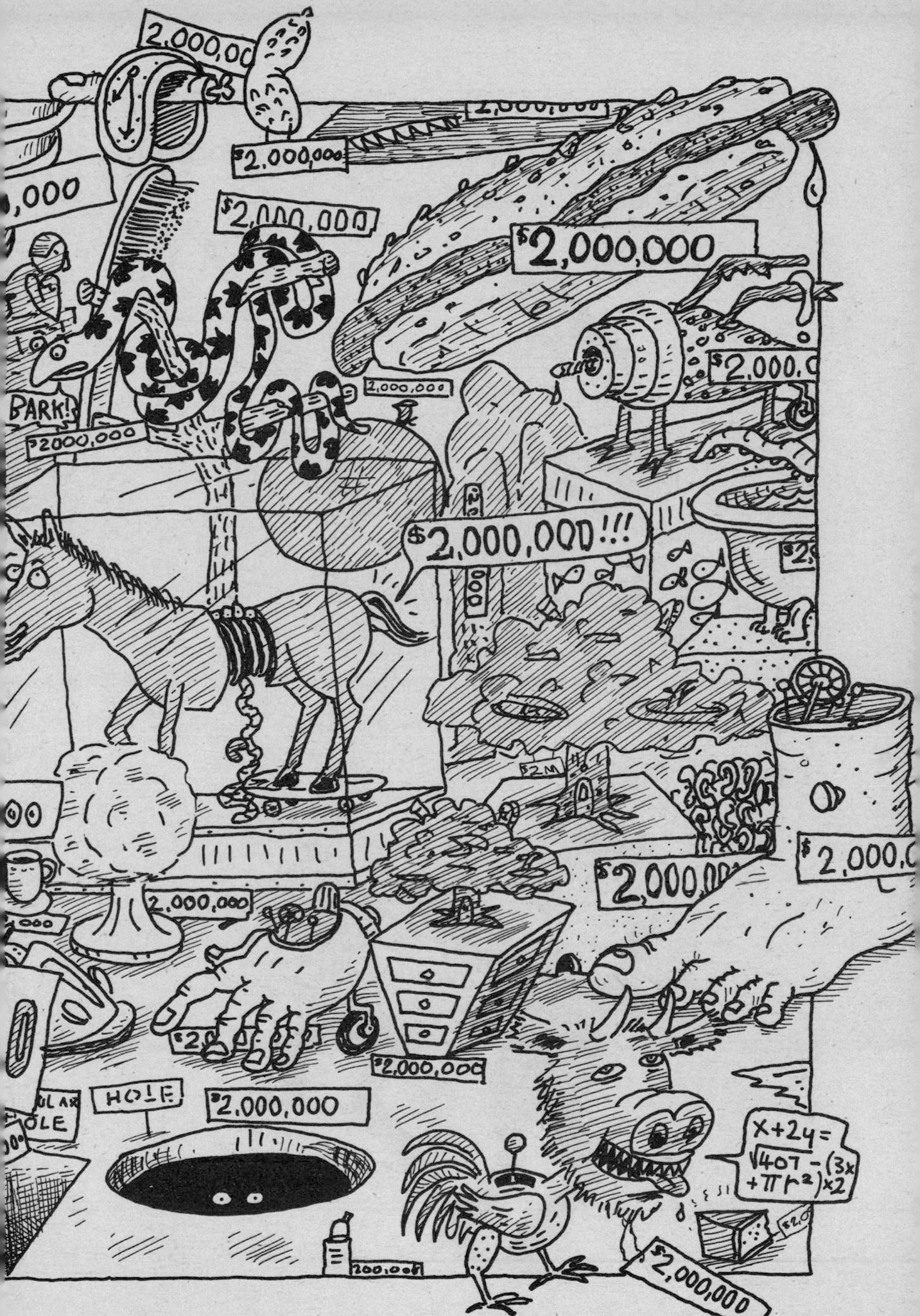
2,000,000
$2,000,000
$2,000,000
$2,000,000
BARK!
$2000,000
2,000,000
$2,000,000!!!
$2M
2,000,000
$2,000,000
HOLE
$2,000,000
x+2y=
√407 − (3x + πr²)×2
200,000
$2,000,000

A Because it's too far to walk.

'Greetings, my good fellows,' says Fancy Fish. 'Welcome to my two-million-dollar emporium. How may I be of service?'

'We'd like to buy a Joke Writer 2000™, please,' I say.

Q What's green, sticky and smells like eucalyptus?

'An excellent choice, if I may say so, sir,' says Fancy Fish. 'The Joke Writer 2000™ is a wonderful pencil and very well-priced at only two million dollars. They have proved enormously popular—in fact, this is my last one.' He places it on the counter in front of us.

'We'll buy it!' says Terry.

'Hang on, not so fast,' I say. I turn to Fancy Fish. 'Will you excuse me for a moment while I consult with my colleague?'

'Of course,' says Fancy Fish.

I draw Terry aside.

'What's the matter, Andy?' he says. 'It's exactly what we need.'

'Yes,' I say, 'but it costs two million dollars and we only have two one-dollar coins!'

'Oh, yeah,' says Terry, 'that's too bad … unless …
unless …'

'Unless what?' I say.

'Unless we use our money-making machine to
make one million, nine hundred and ninety-nine
thousand, nine hundred and ninety-eight dollars?
Then we can add our two one-dollar coins and
we'll have two million dollars!'

'Brilliant!' I say. 'Why didn't *I* think of that?'

'Because you've got a toothache, that's why.'

'*Ouch!*' I say. 'Thanks for reminding me.'

I turn to Fancy Fish. 'Hold that Joke Writer 2000™ —we'll be right back!'

'Well, I'll try,' says Fancy Fish, 'but I can't guarantee anything. At this price it won't last long.'

Q   Why do some fish live at the bottom of the ocean?

CHAPTER 4

THE 100-BEAR BUNFIGHT

We hurry to the money-making machine.

'How do you turn this thing on?' I say.

'Easy,' says Terry. 'You just flick the HONEY/
MONEY switch to MONEY and then press the ON
button—like this.'

The machine whirs into action and money starts flying everywhere.

'Making money is fun!' says Terry as he jumps around excitedly, snatching money out of the air.

'Be careful,' I say. 'Don't bump the HONEY/MONEY switch.'

Q   What is harder to catch the faster you run?

'Oops,' says Terry, as he slips backwards and bumps into the HONEY/MONEY switch!

The machine makes a weird growling, gluggy sound as it switches from making money to making …

A   Your breath.

Q What did the bee say to the flower?

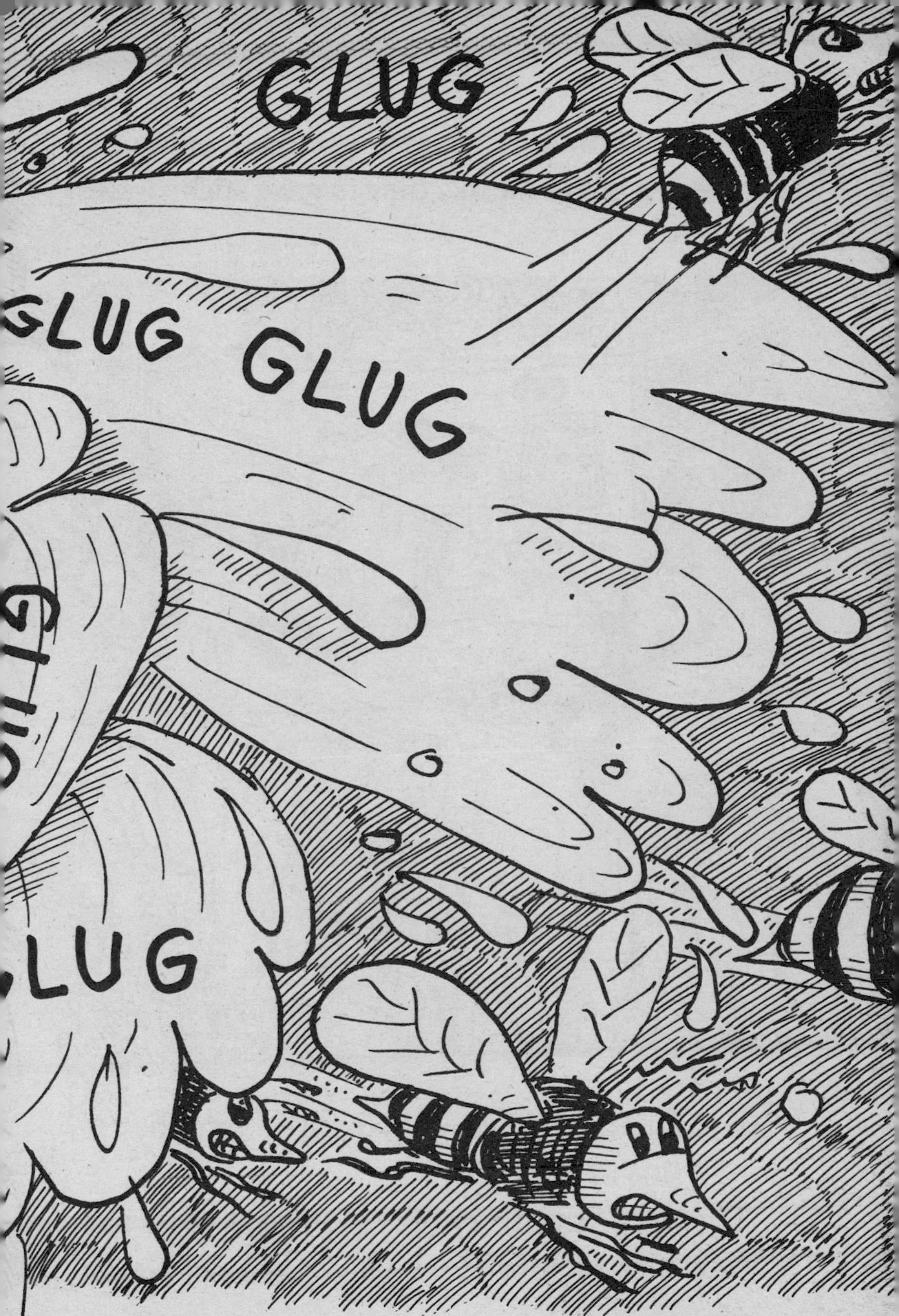
GLUG
GLUG
GLUG
GLUG
LUG

Before we know it, we're up to our knees in honey!
It's pouring out of the machine in great sticky waves.

'Terry, you idiot!' I yell. 'You bumped into the
HONEY/MONEY switch.'

   'I'm sorry,' says Terry. 'But it's okay, I've turned
the machine off now.'

'Then why is it still making that weird growling sound?' I say.

'That's not the machine,' says Terry. 'That's *actual* growling—I think it's coming from all those bears!'

'Bears?' I say.

'Yes,' says Terry. 'Look!'

Q How do bears keep their caves cool?

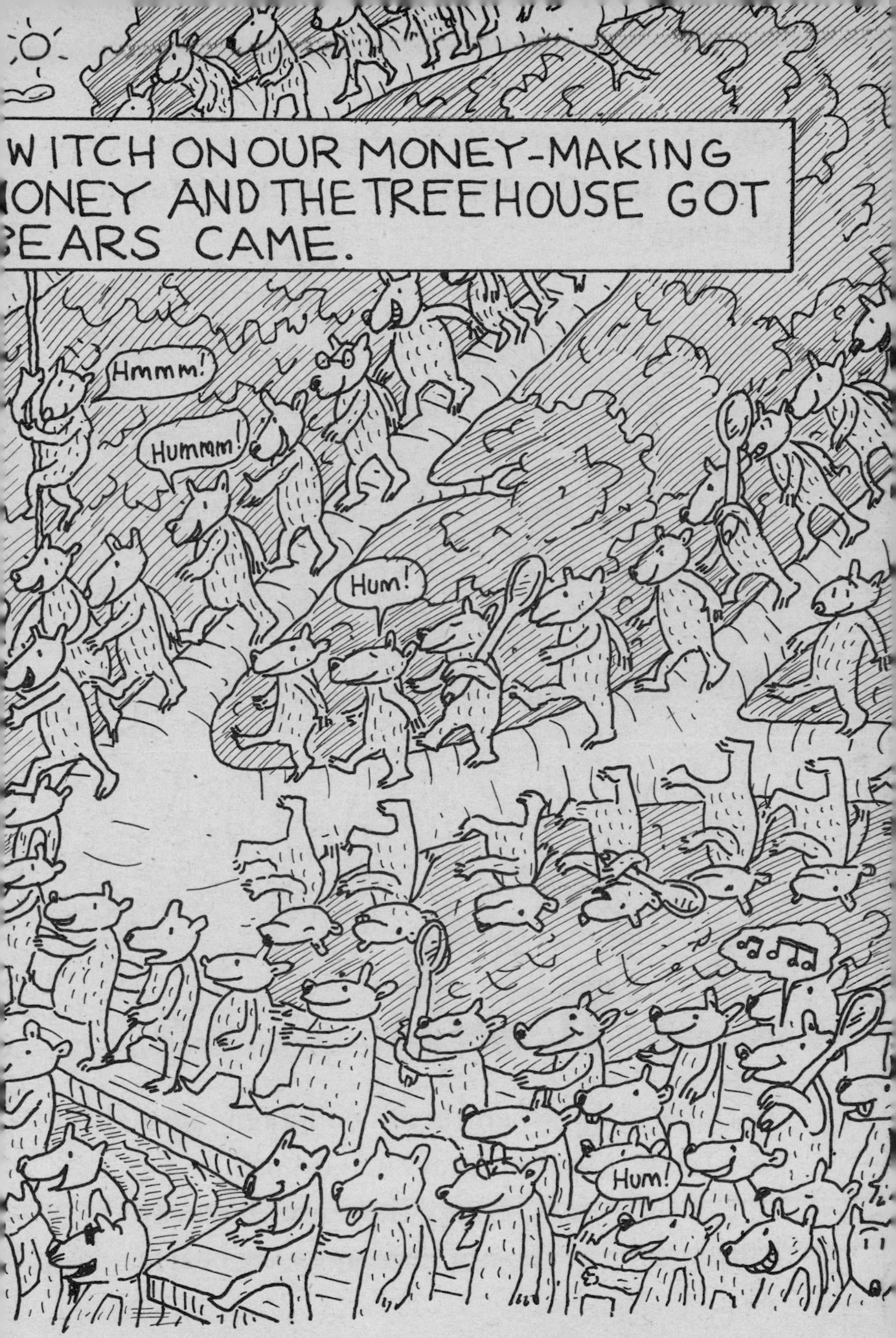
WITCH ON OUR MONEY-MAKING
ONEY AND THE TREEHOUSE GOT
EARS CAME.
Hmmm!
Hummm!
Hum!
Hum!

'Oh, no!' says Terry. 'This is *bad*!'

'No,' I say, 'it's actually *good*—they're eating all the honey!'

'But what about when there's no more honey left?' says Terry. 'Then the bears will eat *us*!'

'Not these ones,' I say. 'These are obviously *honey*-eating bears, not human-eating bears.'

'I think they must be bun-eating bears as well,' says Terry, pointing up at the bunfighting level. 'Look!'

'Uh-oh!' I say. 'They're not just *eating* the buns—they're throwing them as well ...
WATCH OUT!!!'

I take cover but Terry is too slow. One of the buns hits him in the head and knocks him over.

Terry jumps back up. 'Right!' he says. 'This means war!'

'Yeah,' I say. 'If it's a bunfight they want, then it's a bunfight they'll get!'

Q   What do you call a bear with no teeth?

We scoop up the buns the bears have thrown at us and start hurling them back.

Q When are people like bears?

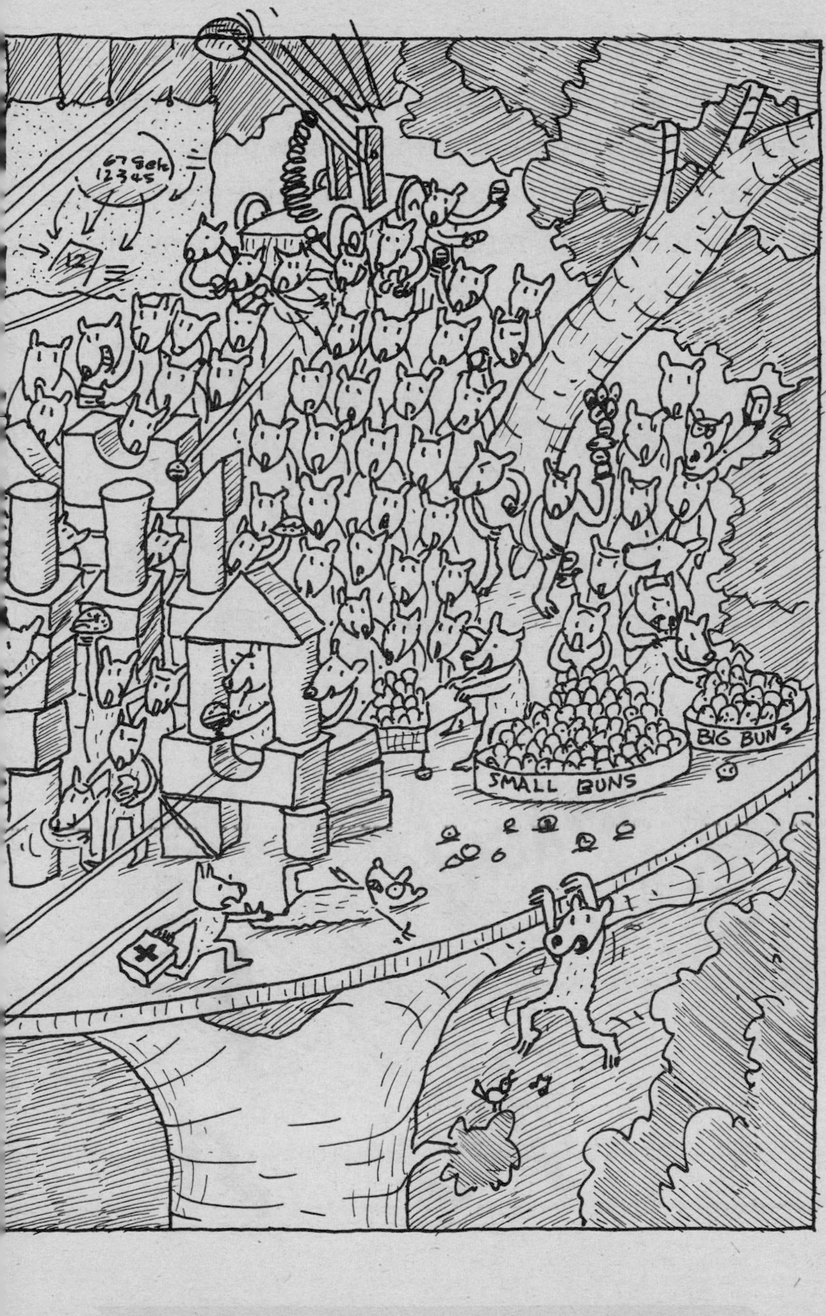
67 8 etc
12345
12
SMALL BUNS
BIG BUNS

A When they're *bare*foot.

Buns of all types are flying through the air in all directions. Hot-cross buns, cold-cross buns, Boston buns, cinnamon buns, cream buns, currant buns, out-of-date buns, hamburger buns, hotdog buns, refrigerator buns … hang on, REFRIGERATOR BUNS?!

Q How far can a bear walk into the woods?

There's no such thing as *refrigerator buns*!
The bears are throwing *actual* refrigerators!

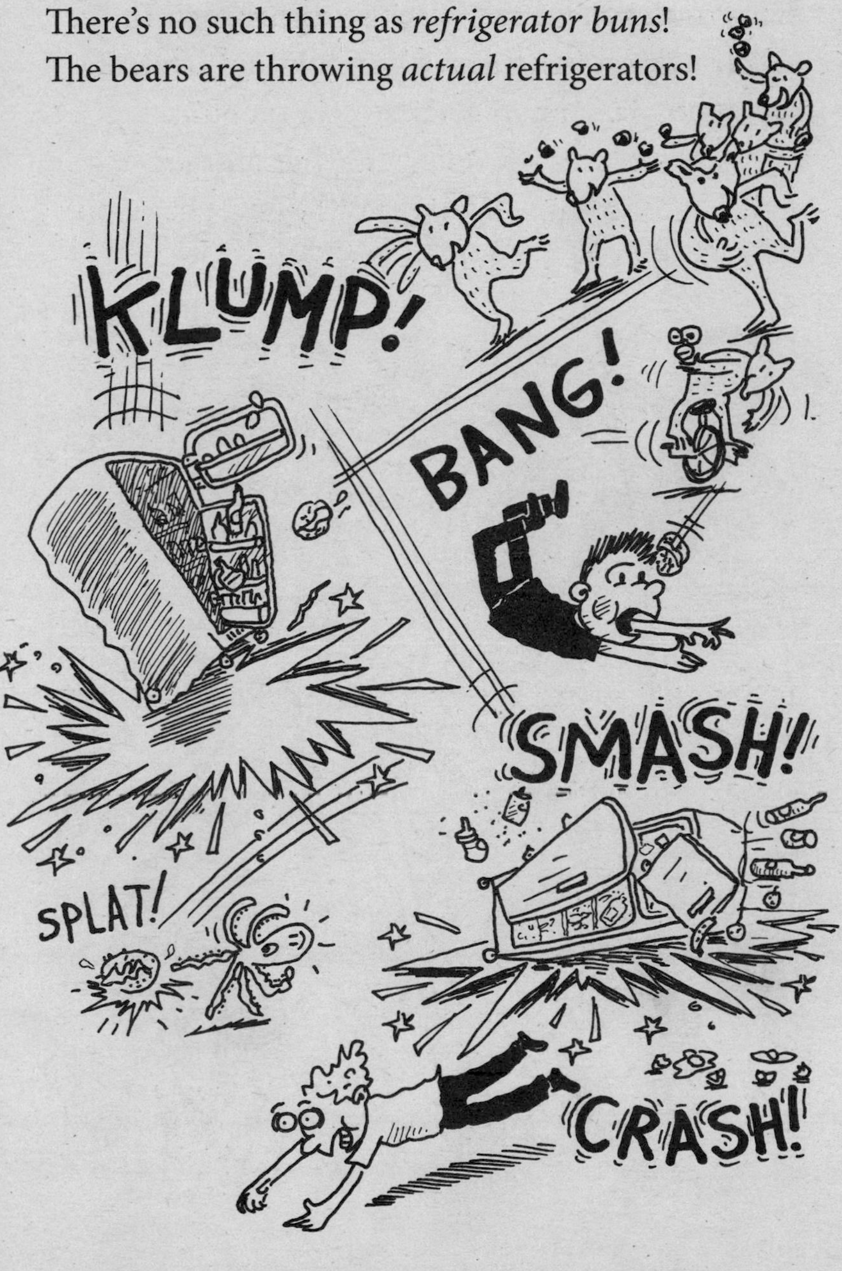
KLUMP!
BANG!
SMASH!
SPLAT!
CRASH!

'Cut it out, you bears!' I say. 'Fridge-throwing is totally against the rules of bunfighting! Look at the sign!'

Q What's black and white, black and white, black and white?

'Maybe bears can't read,' says Terry.

'I think you're right,' I say. 'We'd better get to the fortress—and fast—before we get flattened by a flying fridge!'

'Or four flying fridges,' says Terry, as four flying fridges fly towards us. 'Flee!'

We make it just in time. Fridges smash into the wall of our fortress, but because it's reinforced with extra-strong fortress reinforcer it has no trouble withstanding the ferocious fridge attack.

A A panda bear rolling down a hill.   89

'How long do you think they'll keep it up for?' says Terry.

'Who knows?' I say. 'They could go on forever … or until the refrigerator-vending machine runs out of refrigerators—whichever comes first, I guess.'

'If only Jill was here,' says Terry. 'She could talk to the bears and ask them to stop throwing fridges.'

'Hey, I know,' I say, 'let's call Jill!'

'Good idea, Andy!' says Terry.

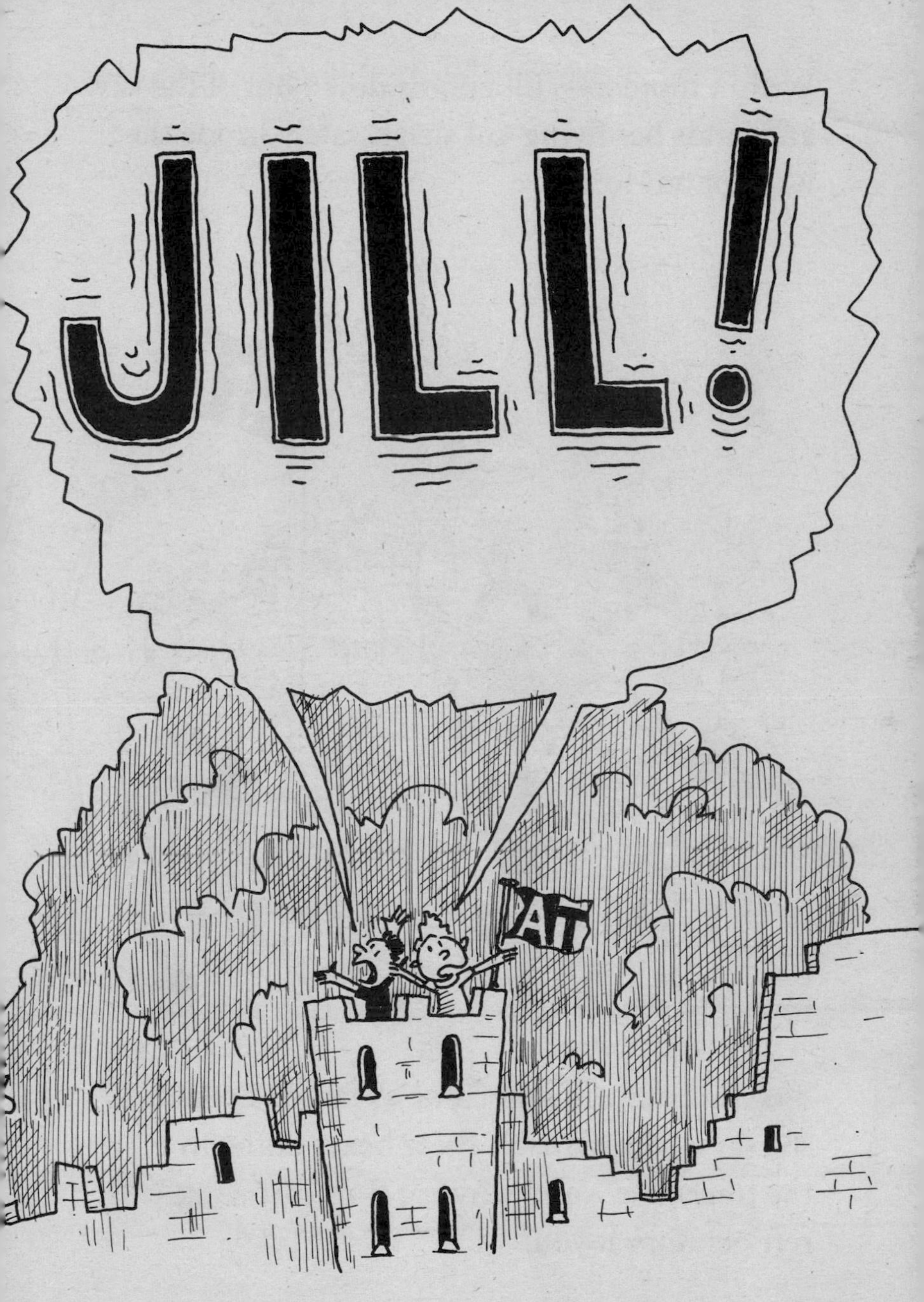
JILL!
AT

Within moments, Jill zooms down out of the sky and lands her flying-cat sleigh safely inside the walls of our fortress.

'I heard your call and came as fast as I could,' she says. 'What are all these bears doing in the treehouse—and why are they throwing refrigerators at you?'

Q Why did the bear fail his maths test?

'Well,' I say, 'we were using the money-making machine to make some money but Terry knocked the switch to HONEY and then the bears came to eat it all up. And then they started throwing buns.'

'And fridges,' says Terry. 'Can you make them stop?'

'Well, I'll try,' says Jill. 'Bears can be very stubborn but I'll have a word with them.'

Q Why did the fridge fall off its bike?

The bears put the fridges down and look up at Jill.

'I'm very disappointed in you bears,' she says. 'This is no way to behave when you're a guest in somebody's treehouse.'

One of the bears steps forward and growls quietly up at Jill.

'That must be their spokesbear,' says Terry.

Jill turns to us. 'The bears say they're very sorry,' she says.

'That's okay,' I say.

'Yeah,' says Terry. 'It's all right. The bunfight was actually a lot of fun. It was just the fridges we had a problem with.'

'You know,' Jill says to the bears, 'it's almost winter so you should be settling down to some serious hibernation. How about you all go home now and I'll come to your cave later, tuck you in and read you a nice bear-time story, perhaps even *The 104-Storey Treehouse*?'

The bears obviously like Jill's idea. They start jumping around excitedly, high-pawing one another.

'Bears *love* their bear-time stories,' explains Jill.

The spokesbear taps Jill on the shoulder and growls in her ear.

Jill turns to us and says, 'He wants to know if there are any bears in your story?'

'Only about one hundred!' I say.

The bears all start growling excitedly and Jill translates for us.

'They said would you please come, too, and read it with me?'

'Sure,' says Terry. 'We can do that.'

'Yes,' I say. 'But we have to finish it first.'

'Well, we'd better get going then,' says Jill, 'and let you get on with it.'

She climbs into her flying-cat sleigh and calls to the bears. 'Follow me! My cats and I will show you the quickest way home.'

'See you all later!' shouts Terry. 'And thanks for eating all the honey—it would have taken us ages!'

CHAPTER 5

IF ONLY ...

'Well, if we're going to have this book ready to read to the bears, we'd better get started,' says Terry.

'I know!' I say (*moan*). 'But my tooth is still killing me. I hope the money-making machine made enough money for us to buy the Joke Writer 2000™.'

I pick up a handful of sticky money and start counting.

'One … five … two … (*groan*)'

'Andy?' says Terry.

'Shush,' I say, 'I'm trying to concentrate. Seven … five … nine … (*moan*)'

Why didn't the cannibals eat the clown?

'Um, Andy?'

'Not now, Terry. Ten ... eleventeen—'

'ANDY!!!' shouts Terry.

'Stop interrupting me!' I say. 'You've made me lose my place! I'm going to have to start all over again!'

'Sorry,' says Terry. 'But that's what I wanted to talk to you about. The readers and I were wondering if you could count a bit faster … and in the right order.'

'I'm counting as fast—and as well—as I can!' I say.

'But it's taking *forever*,' says Terry. 'I think you might need a little help. I'm going to the stupid-hat level—I'll be right back.'

What do penguins wear on their heads?

A few minutes later Terry returns with a stupid-looking hat, which he puts on my head.

'I don't want to wear this stupid hat,' I say.

'I know it looks stupid,' says Terry, 'but it will make you smart: it's a stupid-looking, super-fast counting hat.'

'Well, in that case,' I say, 'let the super-fast counting begin!'

THE DAY I PUT ON THE STUPID-LOOKING, SUPER-FAST COUNTING HA̶ AND COUNTED FASTER THAN ANY PERSON HAS EVER COUNTED IN THE ENTIRE HISTORY OF COUNTING...EVER

1..2...3..4..5..
...15..16..17..18
33...
520

Why was six afraid of seven?

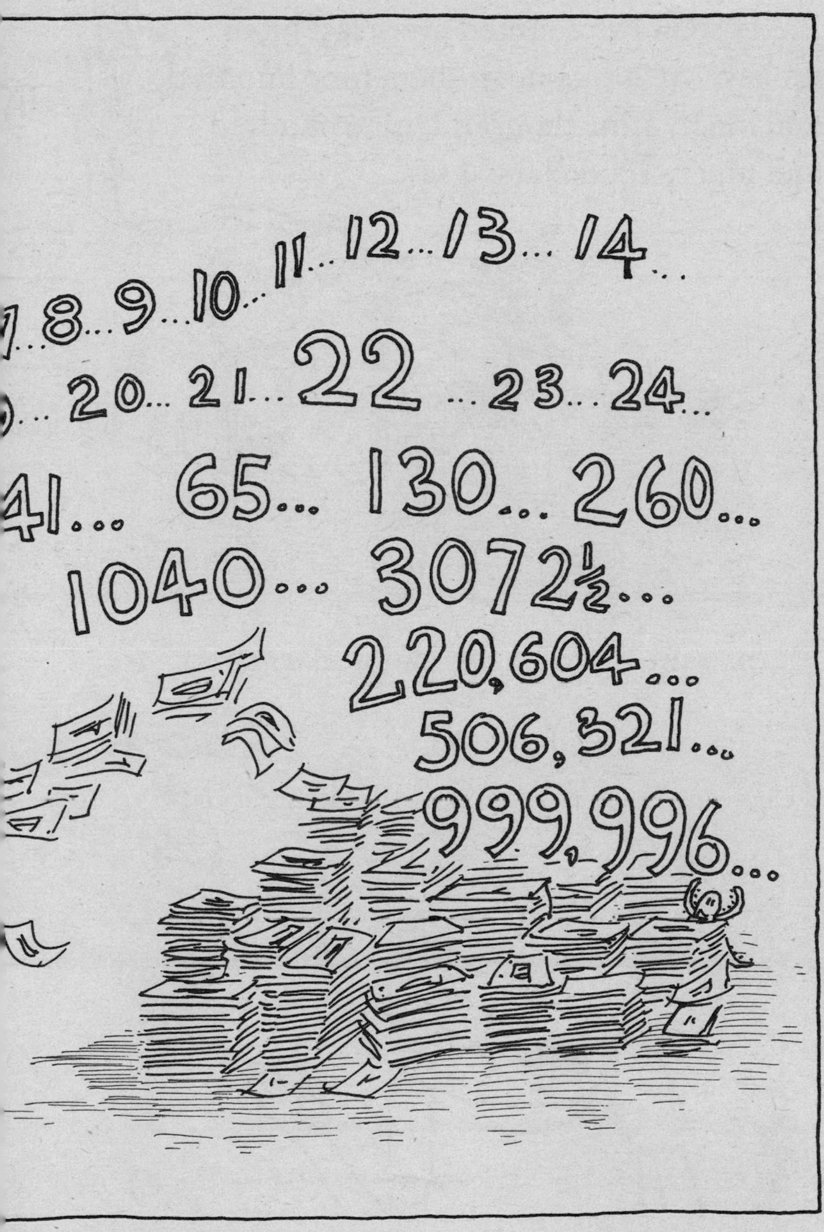
8... 9... 10... 11... 12... 13... 14...
20... 21... 22 ... 23... 24...
41... 65... 130... 260...
1040... 3072½...
220,604...
506,321...
999,996...

A Because seven ate nine.

Pretty soon I've counted every last bit of money. 'We have one million, nine hundred and ninety-nine thousand, nine hundred and ninety-six dollars,' I say.

'Darn!' says Terry. 'We're four dollars short.'

When I point up it's bright but when I point down it's dark. What am I?

'Only *two* dollars short, actually,' I say. 'Remember, we've also got *my* one-dollar coin and *your* one-dollar coin.'

'In that case,' says Terry. 'All we have to do is use the money-making machine to make two more dollars.'

'We can't!' I say. 'The HONEY/MONEY switch is all glugged up with honey and won't flick back to money.'

'Oh, no!' says Terry. 'How are we going to pay for the Joke Writer 2000™ now?'

'I don't know,' I say. 'I can't think of anything. My tooth hurts too much.'

'What about the burp bank?' says Terry. 'We must have at least *twenty* spare burps in there. We could use them!'

'We can't pay in burps,' I say.

'Why not?' says Terry.

'Because then everybody would be doing it,' I say. 'And it would be disgusting.'

'That's too bad,' says Terry. 'I think paying for things with burps would be cool.'

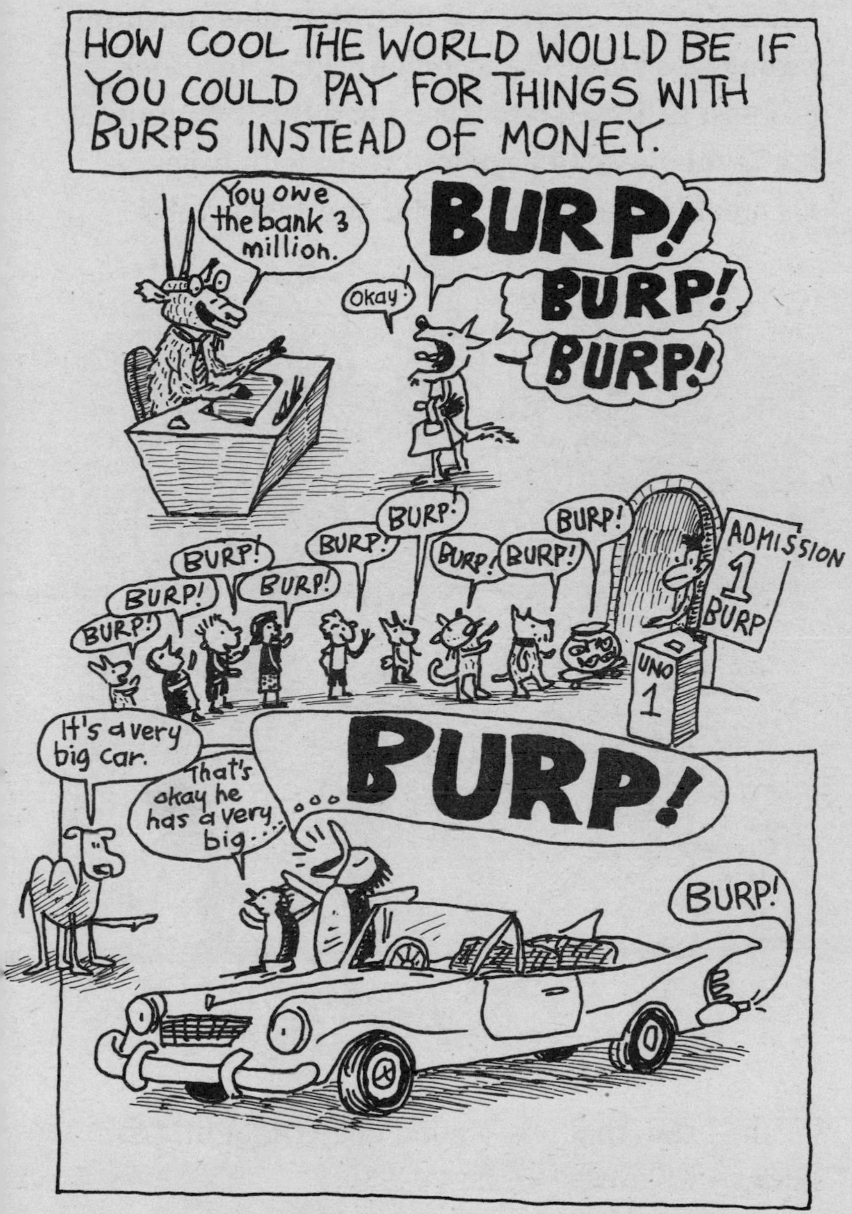
HOW COOL THE WORLD WOULD BE IF YOU COULD PAY FOR THINGS WITH BURPS INSTEAD OF MONEY.
You owe the bank 3 million.
Okay.
BURP!
BURP!
BURP!
BURP!
BURP!
BURP!
BURP!
BURP!
BURP.
BURP!
BURP!
BURP!
BURP!
ADMISSION 1 BURP
UNO 1
It's a very big car.
That's okay he has a very big...
...BURP!
BURP!

A Running out of petrol.

'Maybe we should try the deep-thoughts thinking room,' says Terry. 'That might help. Remember how last time we were there I had the thought that it might be nice to have ice-cream with sausages for breakfast and then we did and I was right?'

'Yeah,' I say, 'that was a good deep thought. Let's try it.'

Two sausages are on a grill. One says, 'Wow, is it hot in here or is it just me?' What does the other one say?

We fly to the deep-thoughts thinking room and settle into our deep-thoughts thinking positions.

'Hmmm (*moan*) …'

'Got anything yet, Andy?'

'Nope. You?'

'Not yet …'

Q   What happened to Einstein when he took a shower?

'Hang on (*groan*), I think
I'm having a deep thought!'

'Hey, me too!
What's yours?'

'It's about how much
my tooth is aching …'

'Mine's about sausages …'

What does a shark eat with peanut butter?

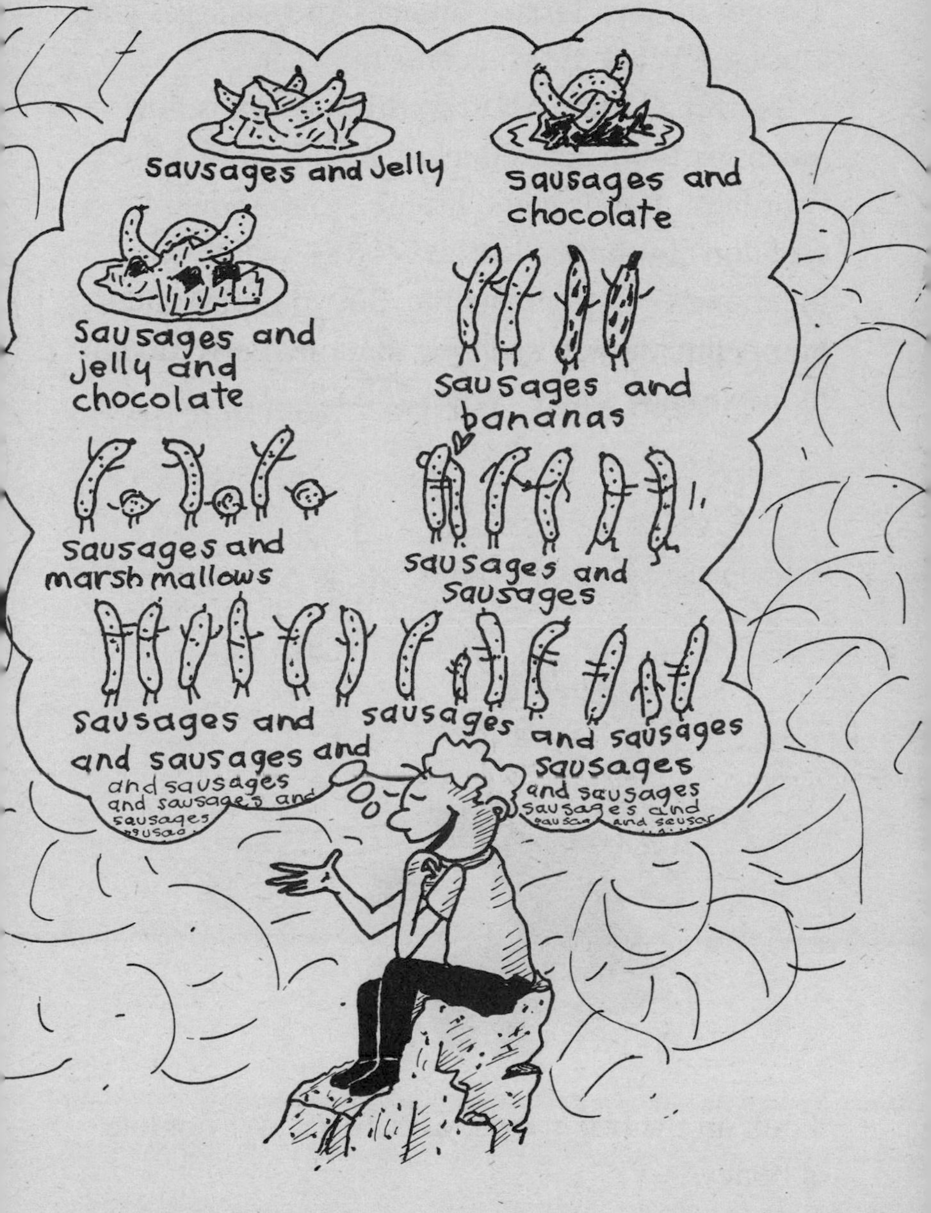
sausages and Jelly
sausages and chocolate
sausages and jelly and chocolate
sausages and bananas
sausages and marshmallows
sausages and sausages
sausages and sausages and sausages and sausages
and sausages and
and sausages
and sausages and
sausages
and sausages
sausages and

A Jellyfish.

'I've got it!' says Terry. 'Sausages and sausages *and* sausages! What did you come up with?'

'Nothing,' I say. 'All I can think about is how much my tooth aches (*moan*). And how it's all your fault! If only you'd listened to me when I said don't bump the HONEY/MONEY switch on the money-making machine. But you went and bumped it anyway and now we don't have enough money to buy a Joke Writer 2000™!'

'Look on the bright side,' says Terry. 'We got lots of honey.'

'But we didn't *need* honey,' I say. 'We need a Joke Writer 2000™! And the only reason we need that is because I have a toothache, and my toothache is *your* fault, too!'

'How is *your* toothache *my* fault?' says Terry.

'Remember that marshmallow-flavoured toothpaste you invented for people who hate peppermint-flavoured toothpaste?'

'Yes,' says Terry. 'What about it?'

'Well, it didn't prevent tooth decay,' I say. 'It *caused* it!'

'That's not my fault,' says Terry, 'I put a warning on the tube. Look—it's right here!'

A   With a tuba toothpaste.

'But why would you invent such a dumb toothpaste in the first place?' I say. 'If only you'd listened to me when I said NOT to invent a really dumb toothpaste! In fact, pretty much *all* of our problems could be avoided IF ONLY YOU WOULD LISTEN TO WHAT I SAY!!!'

'Hey, that gives me an idea for a song,' says Terry.

If only I'd listened to Andy,
I would never have done anything wrong.
If only I'd listened to Andy,
I wouldn't be singing this song.

But I didn't listen to Andy
And now he is groaning in pain.
Oh, why am I always so stupid?
Again and again and again?!

♪ Like the time I married a mermaid,
Who was actually a monster from the sea,
And she practically ended up eating
Both my good friend Andy and me! ♫

Q Which part of a mermaid weighs the most?

And the time I used the sharks in the
  shark tank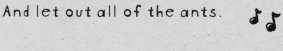
To wash my underpants.
And the time I left open the ant farm gate
And let out all of the ants.

A Her scales.

If only I'd listened to Andy,
I wouldn't have invented a machine
To write and draw our books for us
That turned out to be really mean.

And if only I hadn't trained Ninja Snails—
Oh, hang on, they worked out okay!
Even though it took them 100 years,
They ended up saving the day.

A They use snail polish.

But I didn't listen to Andy
When he warned me about spying cows!
And then their stupid, dumb mooo-vie
Was much more successful than ours.

Q   What do you call a cow's bedtime stories?

♪♪

If only I'd listened to Andy
When we were using our machine
  to make money,
I wouldn't have bumped the switch ♫
And flooded the treehouse with honey.

And **I** would NEVER have invented
   a toothpaste
That was ninety-nine per cent candy.
I'm so sorry for all the dumb things
   I have done.
Oh, **I** feel so bad for poor Andy.

Q   How do you spell candy in two letters?

If only I could think of a way
To get that tooth out of his head,
Why, I'd pull it right out in an instant
And he could leave it at night by his bed.

The tooth fairy could come and collect it
And leave a gold coin in its place
And Andy would feel so much better—
It would put a huge smile on his face!

He'd say, 'Terry, you're not such a dumdum!
You've done something right for a change!
We can take all this money back to the shop
And get the pencil we need in exchange!'

'THAT'S IT! HEY, ANDY! I'VE GOT A WAY TO SOLVE ALL OUR PROBLEMS AND MAKE EVERYTHING RIGHT!'

Q What happens when you put a tooth into a glass of water?

'Not now, Terry,' I say. 'This is no time for jokes—my tooth is hurting too much!'

'I know that,' he says, 'but your tooth is the solution to our problem.'

'How do you figure that?' I say.

'All we need to do is pull it out,' says Terry. 'And then you can leave it out tonight for the tooth fairy and you will get two dollars for it and then we'll have enough money to buy the Joke Writer 2000™!'

'That's crazy,' I say.

'Oh,' says Terry, disappointed.

'*So* crazy it just might work!' I say. 'Let's try it!'

'Yay!' says Terry.

CHAPTER 6

TUG OF WAR

'Terry Dent*ist* at your service!' says Terry. 'Hold still and I'll just knock your tooth out with this hammer.'

'No way!' I say. 'It's hurting enough already! No hammer!'

A   He nailed it.

'No hammer? No problem!' says Terry. 'I'll use this tooth dynamite instead. It says here: *Just put one stick in your mouth near the aching tooth and light the fuse.*'

'DEFINITELY NOT!' I say. 'No hammer and no tooth dynamite! The tooth fairy won't want my tooth if it's exploded to bits. You are a *terrible* dentist!'

'Well, I'm all out of ideas then,' says Terry. 'Maybe we should go and ask the three wise owls how to get your tooth out.'

'I don't know about that,' I say. 'I'm not so sure those owls are as wise as you think they are.'

'Do you have any other ideas?' says Terry.

'No,' I say with a groan. 'Let's go and see the wise owls.'

We jet-chair up to the owl house.

'Greetings, O wise owls!' says Terry.

Q   What is an owl's favourite subject?

'Just as I suspected,' I say. 'This is a waste of time. Let's go.'

'No, give them a chance, Andy,' says Terry. 'We haven't even asked our question yet.'

Terry turns to address the owls. 'O wise owls! We do beseech thee to tell us the answer to our question: what is the best way to remove Andy's aching tooth?'

'String! Doorknob! Slam!' say the wise owls.

'See?' I say. 'I *knew* this wasn't a good idea. They're just hooting random words!'

'No, they're not!' says Terry. 'They're making perfect sense. They're telling us that all we have to do is tie a bit of *string* to your tooth, tie the other end to a *doorknob* and then *slam* the door. The force of the door slamming will pull out your tooth and all our problems will be solved!'

'Well,' I say, 'it does sound a little less painful than hammers or dynamite.'

'Definitely,' says Terry. 'And we can get some string from the tangled-up level. Come on!' He turns to the wise owls. 'Farewell, O wise ones, and thanks for the wise advice!'

The tangled-up level looks even more tangled-up than usual. It's a big crazy jumble of cords, wires, cables, ribbons, twine, ropes, threads and string all tangled together in the biggest tangled-up tangle you've ever seen. There is caution tape around it but you can't really read it because the caution tape is all tangled up as well.

'I'm going to go in and untangle a bit of string,' says Terry.

'All right,' I say, 'but be careful. It's pretty tangly in there.'

'Don't worry, Andy,' says Terry. 'I'll be really, REALLY careful ...'

Q What boy wizard magically grew a beard each night?

'Help, Andy!' says Terry. 'I'm all tangled up!'

'If only you'd listened to me,' I say. 'I told you to be careful!'

'I *did* listen to you and I *was* careful,' says Terry. 'But I got all tangled up anyway.'

'Well, stop struggling,' I say, 'you're just making it worse. Stay still while I get the emergency detangler.'

I grab the detangler, release the safety catch, point the nozzle at Terry and press the trigger.

Q How does the man in the moon cut his hair?

The detangler has an instant effect.

Every single bit of string, cord, wire, rope and thread is detangled—including Terry's hair, which has gone all straight and is hanging down over his face.

'I can't see!' says Terry. 'I can't see *anything*! Where has everything *gone*?!'

'Calm down,' I say. 'It's just your hair. The detangler has straightened out your curls. Come with me to the giant hairdryer and we'll have you back to normal in no time.'

Q What is good for a bald head?

'Thanks, Andy,' says Terry. 'That feels *much* better!'

'No problem,' I say. 'Did you get the string?'
'String?' says Terry. 'What string?'
'THE STRING YOU WENT TO THE
TANGLED-UP LEVEL TO GET!' I yell.

'Oops,' says Terry. 'After all the tangling and detangling I kind of forgot. But it doesn't matter. I think there's some string in the kitchen drawer.'

'But if you *knew* there was string in the kitchen drawer, why didn't we just get it from there in the first place?'

'Because I forgot,' says Terry. 'I was having a bad hair day, you know.'

'Your bad hair happened *after* you forgot about the string,' I say.

'Oh, yeah,' says Terry. 'I forgot about that, too.'

I groan.

'Poor Andy,' says Terry. 'You sure are in a lot of pain.'

'Let's just go to the kitchen,' I say.

In the kitchen, Terry opens the third drawer down and pulls out a big ball of string.

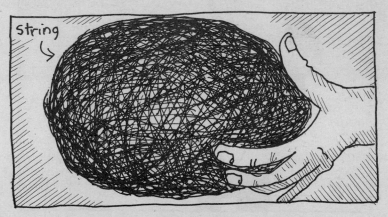

'Open wide, Andy,' he says.

I open my mouth and Terry ties one end of the string to my sore tooth …

and the other end to the handle of our bathroom door.

Imagine you are in a room with no doors, windows or anything. How do you get out?

'Okay,' says Terry. 'Here we go. Ready, set …
SLAM!'
He slams the door.

Q When is a door not a door?

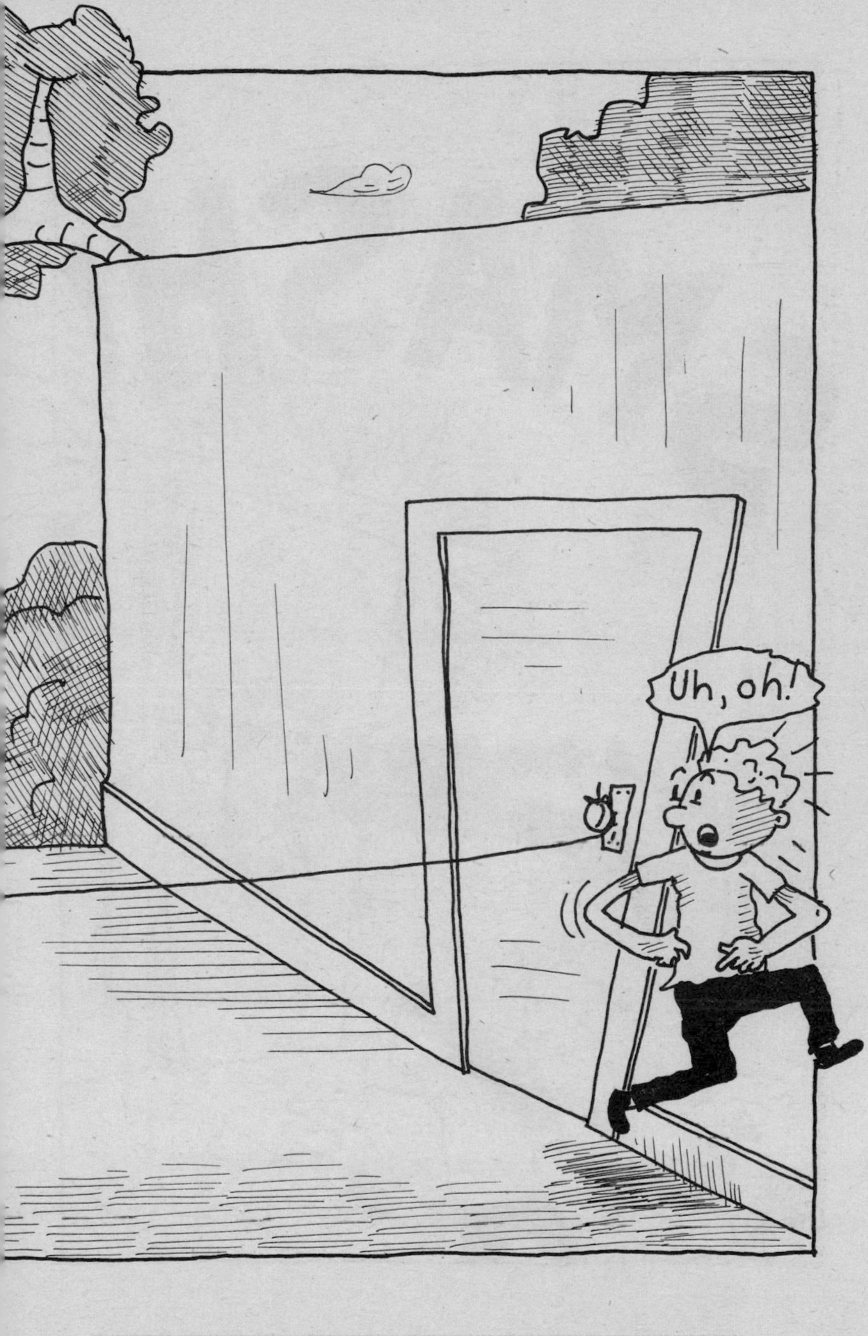
Uh, oh!

A When it's ajar.

What lets you walk through walls?

'Is it out?' says Terry.

'No,' I say. 'And now I've not only got a toothache, I've got a headache as well! This is the worst day ever!'

'Don't despair,' says Terry. 'I think I know another way to do it, but we're going to need some help.'

'It better not involve another door,' I say.

'No,' says Terry. 'Your tooth is too tough for that. It's going to take a full-scale tug of war to get it out of your head. Come with me to the forest.'

Five minutes later we're in the forest. Terry has tied me to a tree and assembled a huge tug-of-war team, including Bill the postman, Edward Scooperhands, the Trunkinator and all of Jill's animals.

Moo!

Neigh!

Why did the scientist put a knocker on her door?

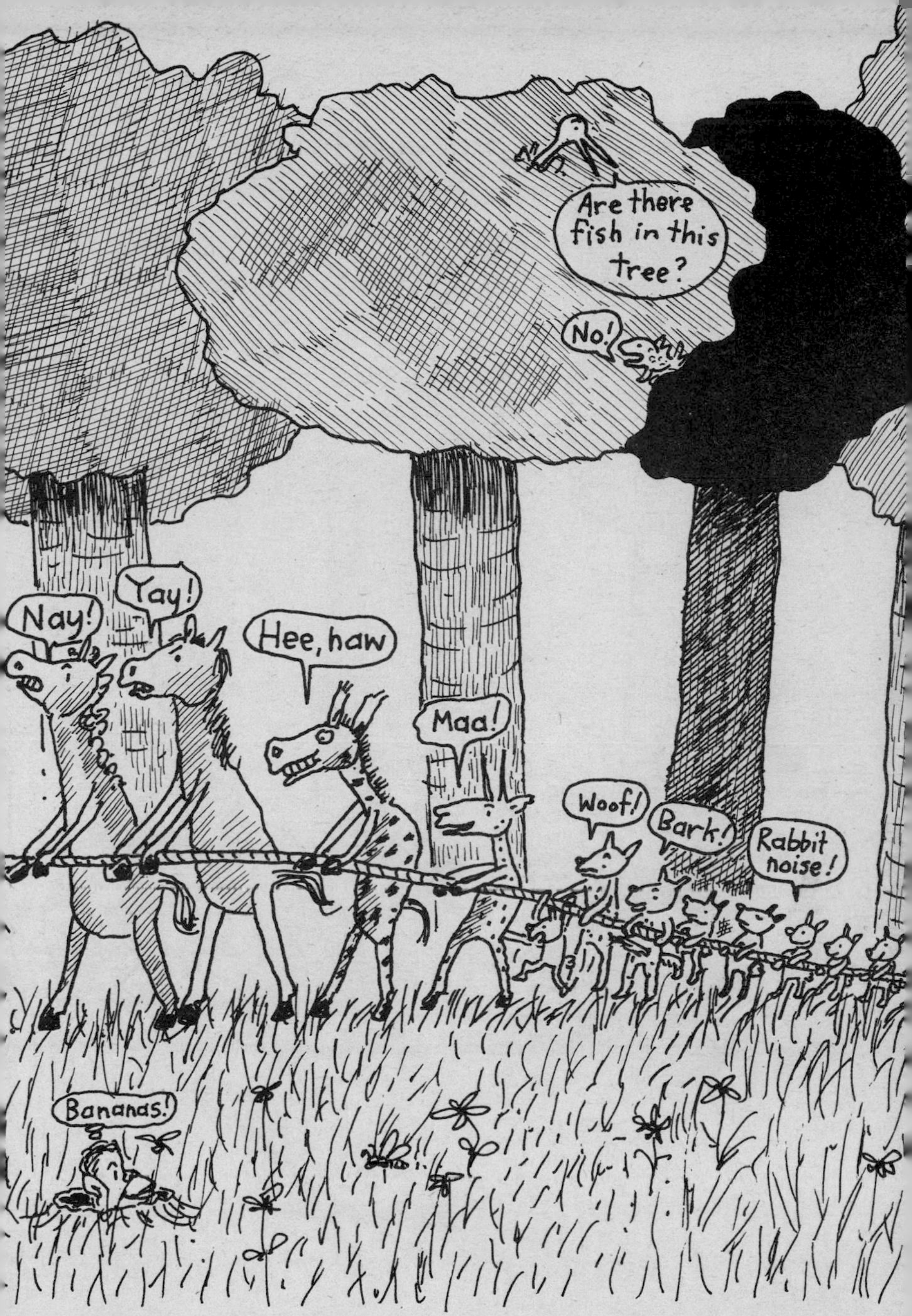
Are there fish in this tree?
No!
Nay!
Yay!
Hee, haw
Maa!
Woof!
Bark!
Rabbit noise!
Bananas!

A Because she wanted the No-bell prize.

In what sport do winners go backwards and losers go forwards?

'Okay,' shouts Terry. 'Here we go! Ready, set … PULL!'

What did the dog say to the little child pulling its tail?

Giant Rabbit

A   'This is the end of me.'

'Aarghh!' I scream, as my tooth is torn out of my mouth.

Q What bird is with you at every meal?

The tug-of-war team, surprised by their sudden victory, lose their grip on the string and all fall backwards in a big heap. My tooth flies upwards, trailing the string behind it …

A   A swallow.

and is snatched by a passing bird!

'Hey!' I say. 'That stupid bird just snatched my tooth!'

'That's not a stupid bird!' says Jill, peering up at it through her birdwatching binoculars. 'That's an extremely rare high-flying, mountain-dwelling worm-snatcher. It must have thought the string was a worm.'

'If it can't tell the difference between a bit of string and a worm, then it *is* a stupid bird,' I say.

'We've got to get Andy's tooth back,' says Terry. 'We need it for the tooth fairy!'

A A bagel.

'Oh, dear,' says Jill, still looking through her binoculars. 'I think that's going to be a bit difficult because the bird is heading for its nest high on a rocky, snow-covered crag near the top of Mount Everest.'

'Well, we'll just have to climb up and get it then, won't we?' I say.

What is green and pecks on trees?

'But we can't climb Mount Everest!' says Terry. 'It's too cold, too high and too hard. Plus, it will take much too long!'

'I'm not suggesting we climb the *mountain*,' I say. 'We'll take the stairs. Our never-ending staircase goes pretty close to the nest. We can climb up, jump across and get the tooth—easy!'

'What are we waiting for then?' says Terry. 'Let's go!'

'I'll come, too,' says Jill. 'I've always wanted to see a high-flying, mountain-dwelling worm-snatcher up close!'

Q Who can jump higher than the highest mountain?

CHAPTER 7

UP AND UP AND UP

We go to the never-ending staircase and start climbing. We climb up and up and ...

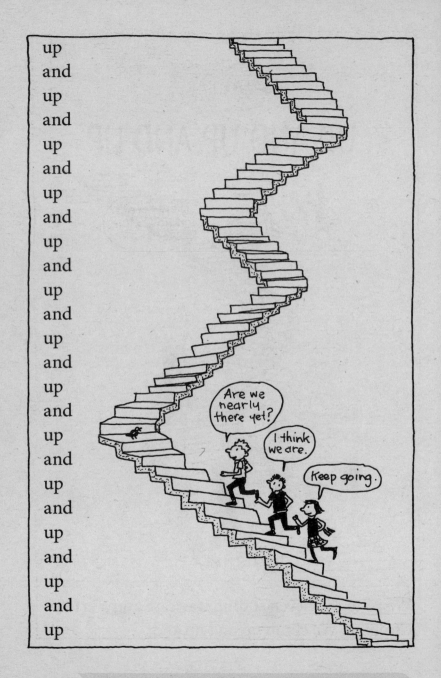

There is a one-storey house where everything is red.

and
up
and
up
and
up
and
up
and
up
and
up
and
up
and
up
and
up
and
up
and
up
and
up
and

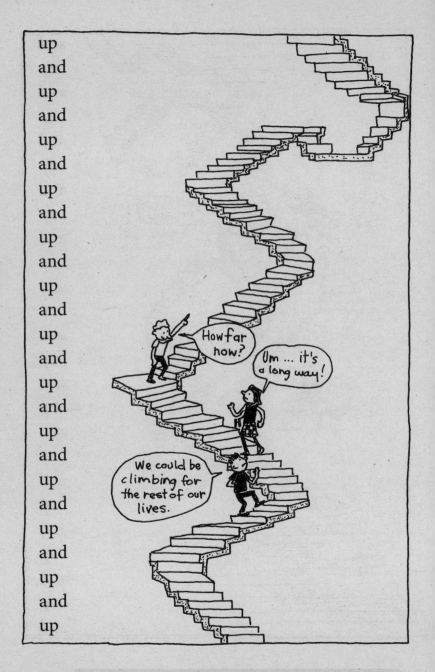

the couch is red, the kitchen is red, the kitchen table is

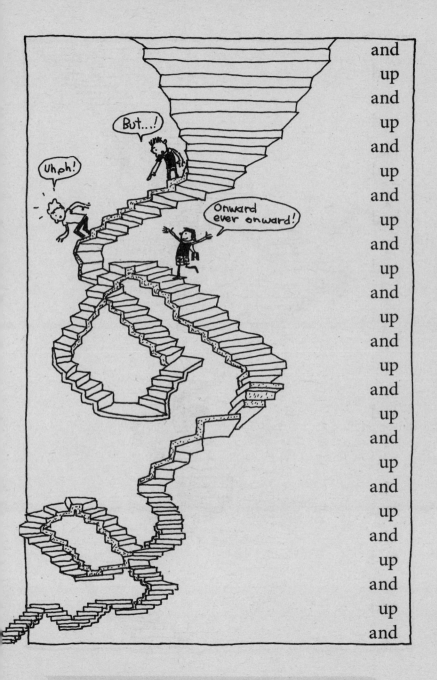

and
up
and
up
and
up
and
up
and
up
and
up
and
up
and
up
and
up
and
up
and
up
and
up
and

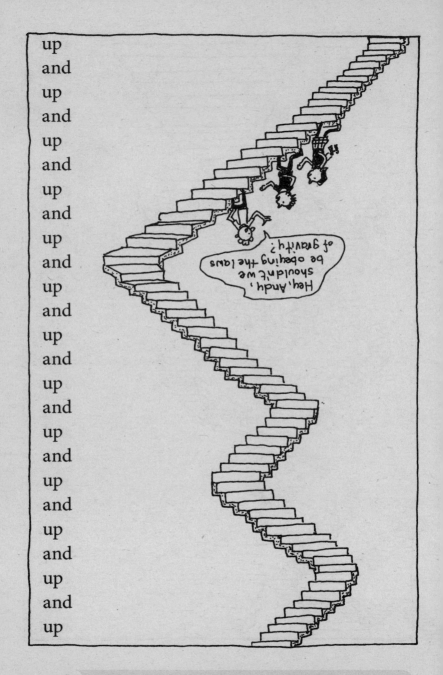

up
and
up
and
up
and
up
and
up
and
up
and
up
and
up
and
up
and
up
and
up
and
up
and
up
and
up

food inside the fridge is red, the calendar on the

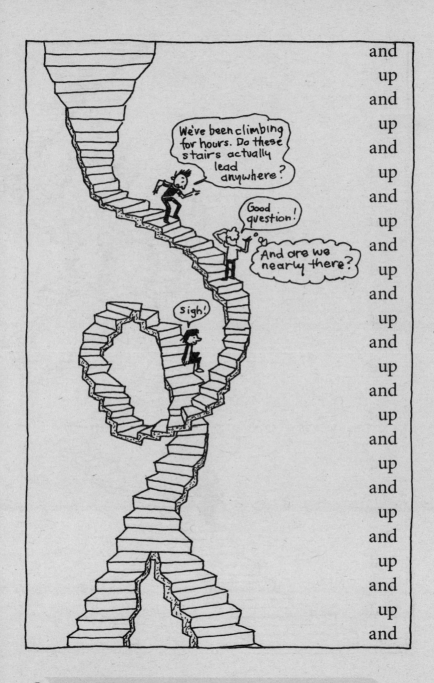

Q wall is red, the clock is red, the knife-block is red …

up
and
up
and
up
and
up
and
up
and
up
and
up
and
up
and
up
and
up
and
up
and
up
and
up
and
up
and
up

the knives are red, the forks are red, the spoons are red,

and
up
and
up
and
up
and
up
and
up
and
up
and
up
and
up
and
up
and
up
and
up
and
up
and

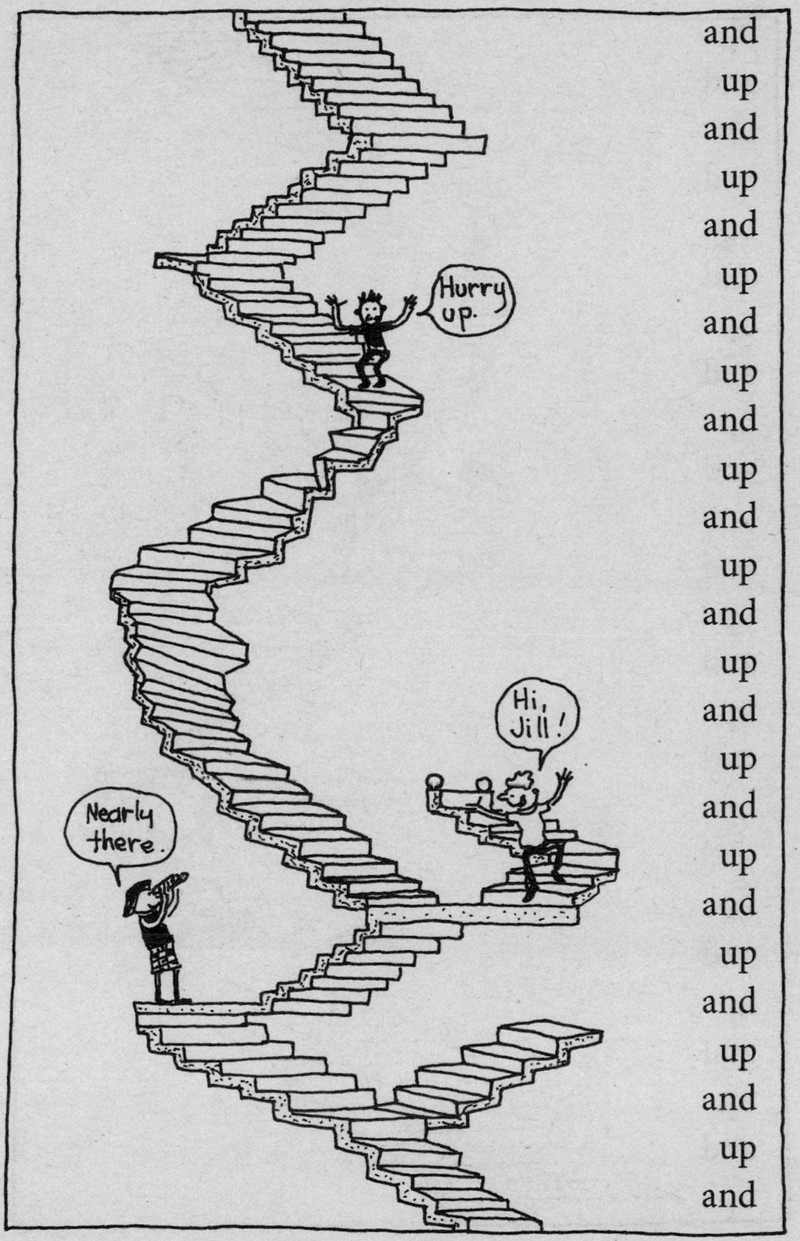
Hurry up.
Hi, Jill!
Nearly there.

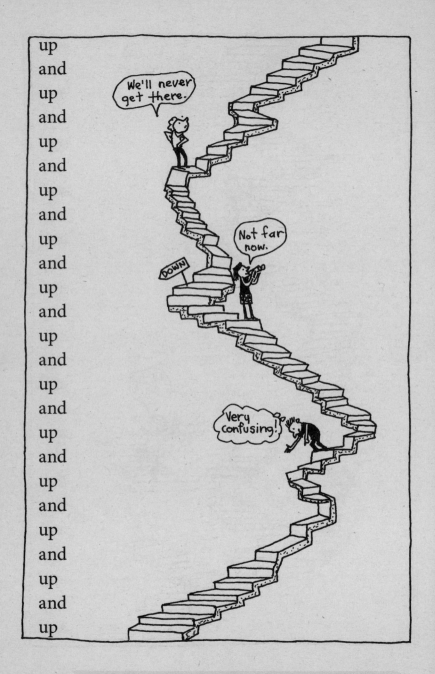

inside them are red—believe it or not, even the dog is red.

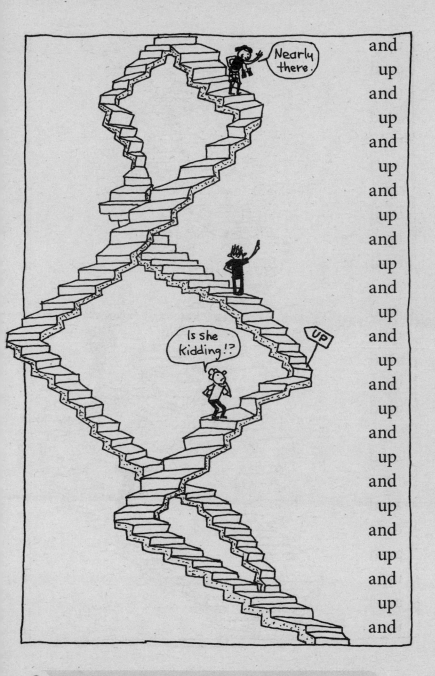

and
up
and
up
and
up
and
up
and
up
and
up
and
up
and
up
and
up
and
up
and
up
and
up
and

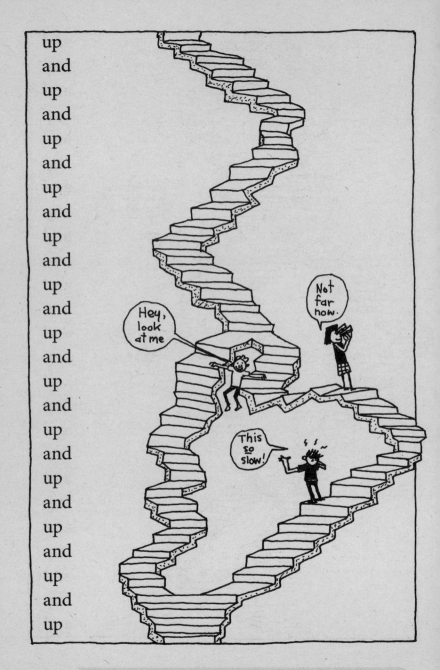

are red, the television is red, even the programs on the

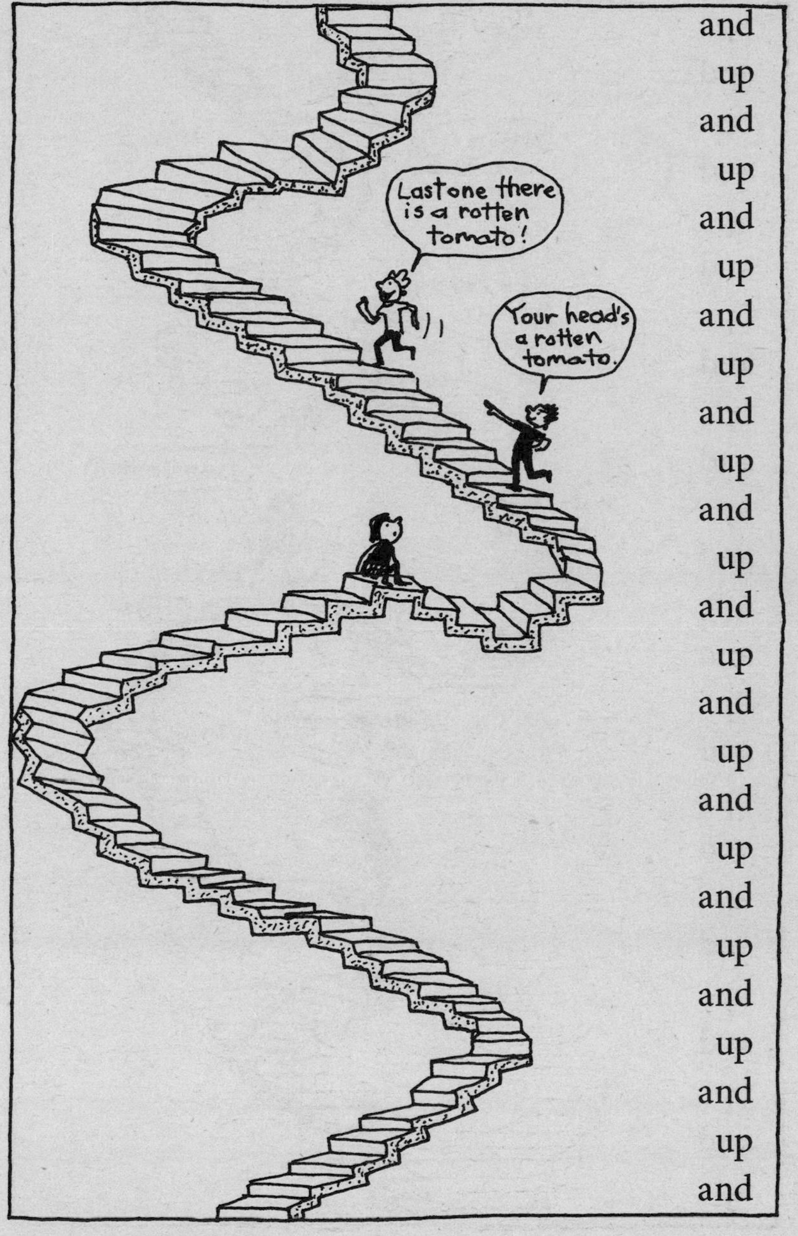
Last one there is a rotten tomato!
Your head's a rotten tomato.

and
up
and
up
and
up
and
up
and
up
and
up
and
up
and
up
and
up
and
up
and
up
and
up
and

up
and
up
and
up
and
up
and
up
and
up
and
up
and
up
and
up
and
up
and
up
and
up
and
up
and
up
and
up
and
up

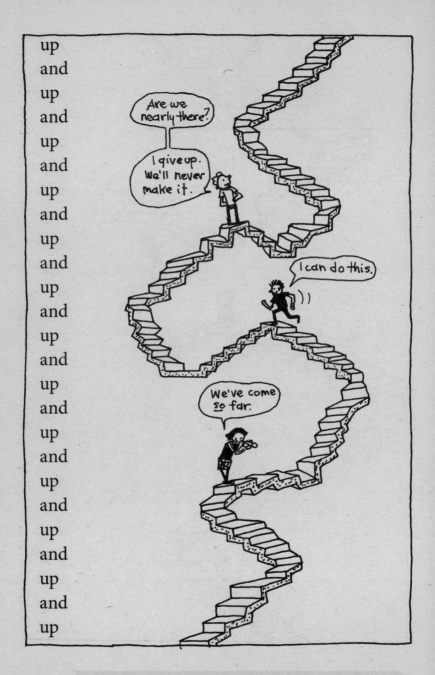

red, the toilet water is red, the toilet brush is red, the

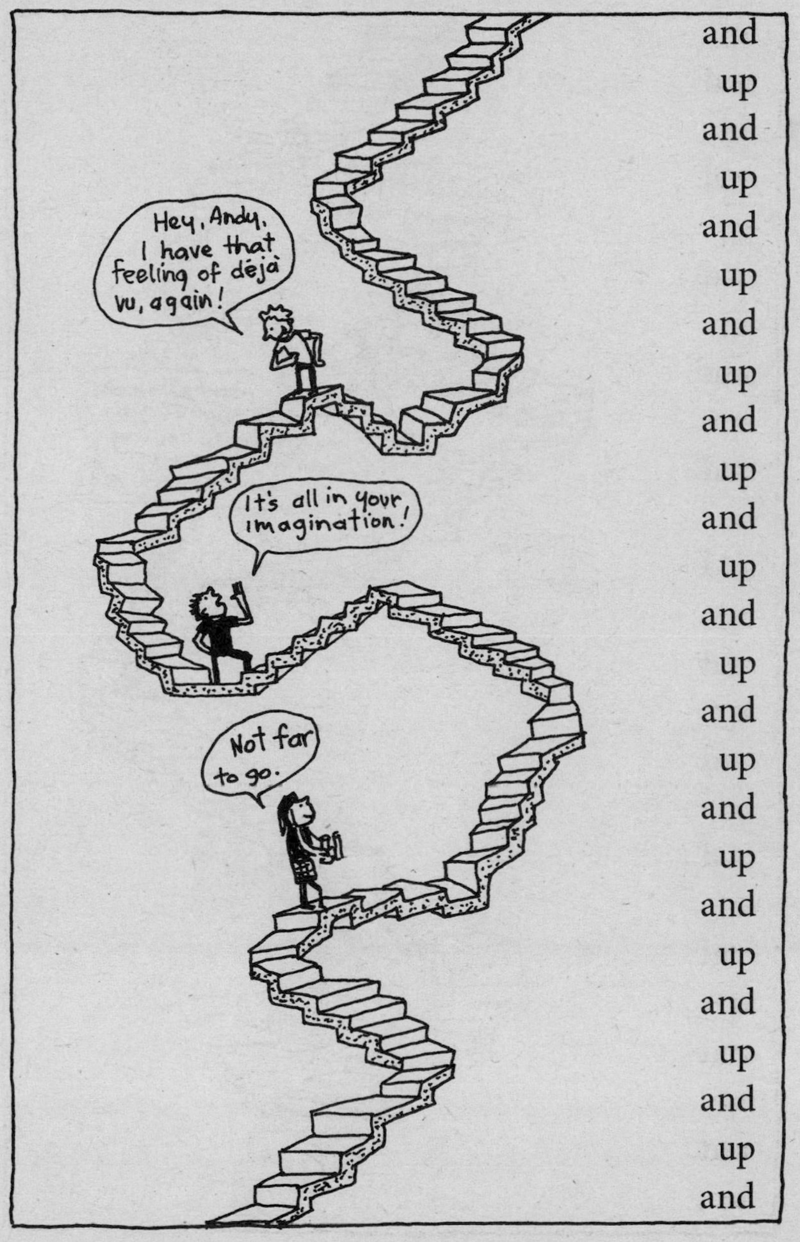
Hey, Andy, I have that feeling of déjà vu, again!
It's all in your imagination!
Not far to go.

and
up
and
up
and
up
and
up
and
up
and
up
and
up
and
up
and
up
and
up
and
up
and

mirrors are red, the basins are red, the taps are red ...

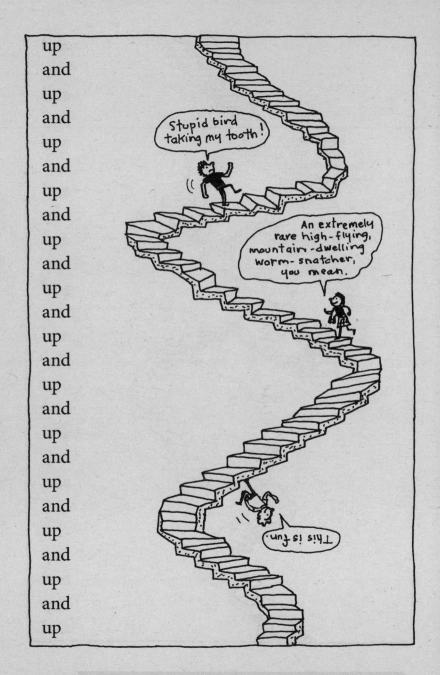

the toothbrushes are red, the toothpaste is red, the

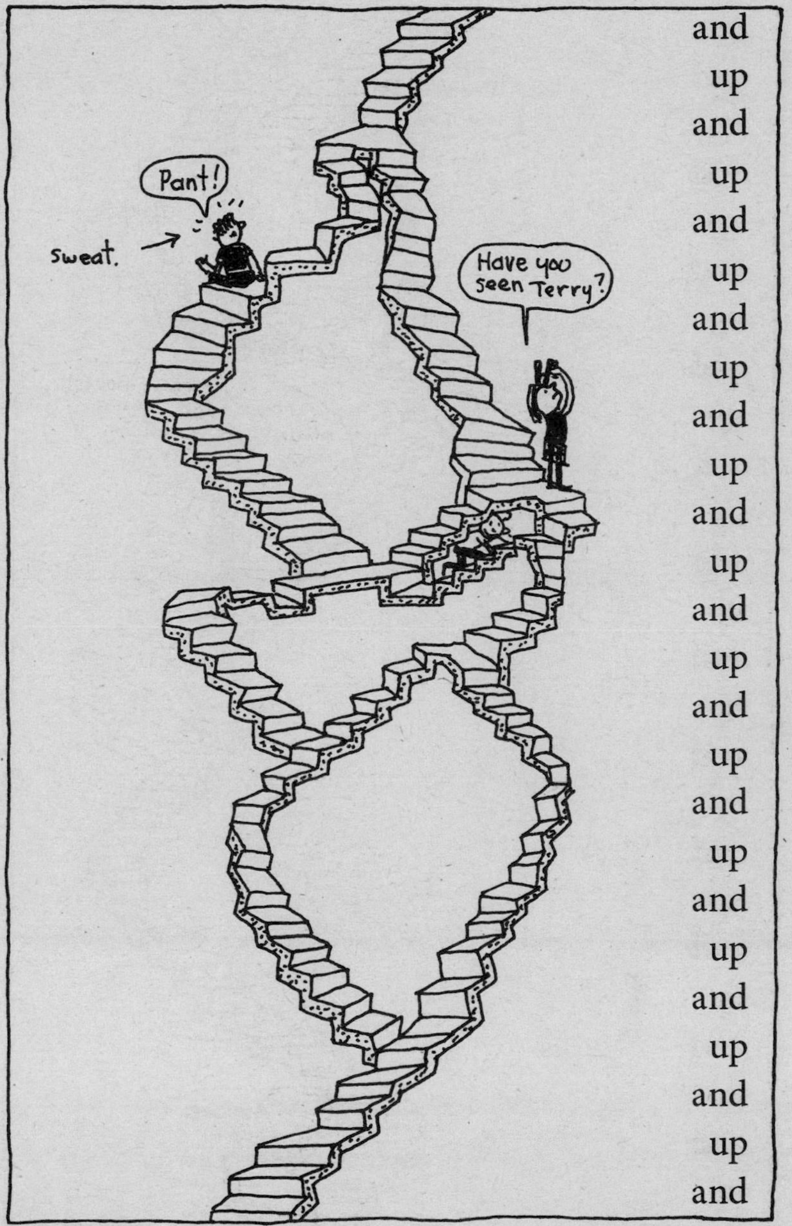
Pant!
sweat.
Have you seen Terry?

and
up
and
up
and
up
and
up
and
up
and
up
and
up
and
up
and
up
and
up
and
up
and
up
and

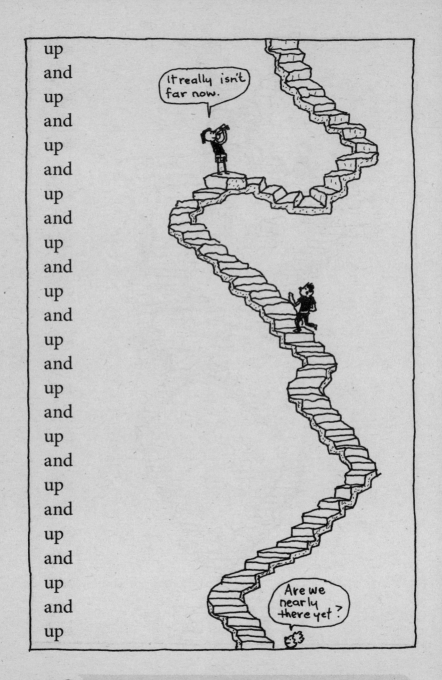

the hallway is red, the air is red, the bookshelves are

and
up
and
up
and
up
and
up
and
up
and
up
and
up
and
up
and
up
and
up
and
up
and

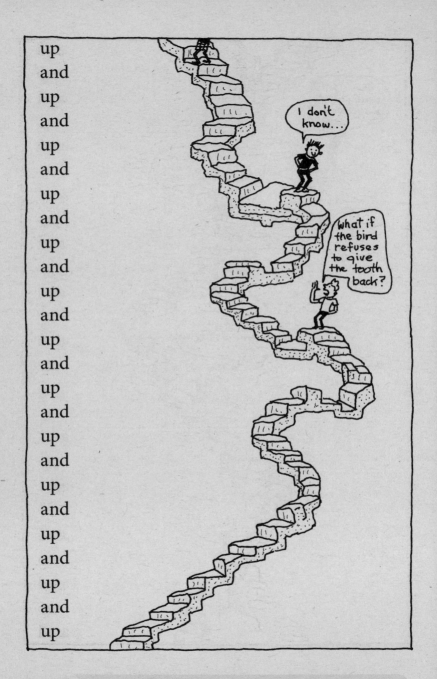

of the books are red, the words are red, the letters are

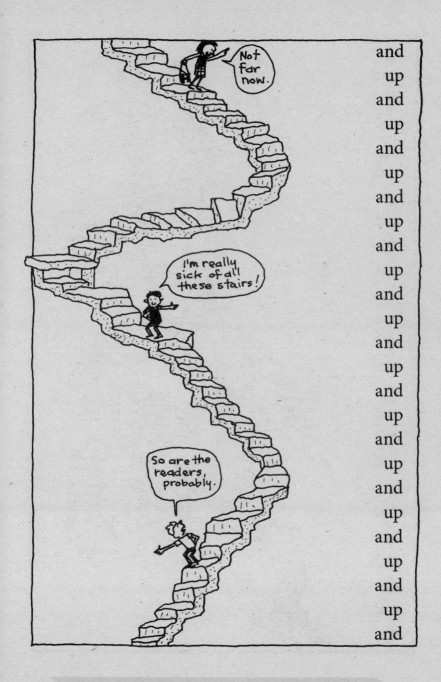

and
up
and
up
and
up
and
up
and
up
and
up
and
up
and
up
and
up
and
up
and

up
and
up
and
up
and
up
and
up
and
up
and
up
and
up
and
up
and
up
and
up
and
up
and
up
and
up
and
up

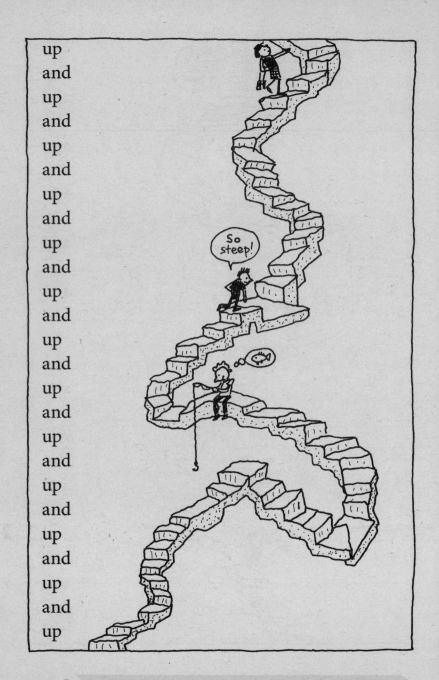

are red, the curtains are red, the dining table is red,

and
up
and
up
and
up
and
up
and
up
and
up
and
up
and
up
and
up
and
up
and
up
and

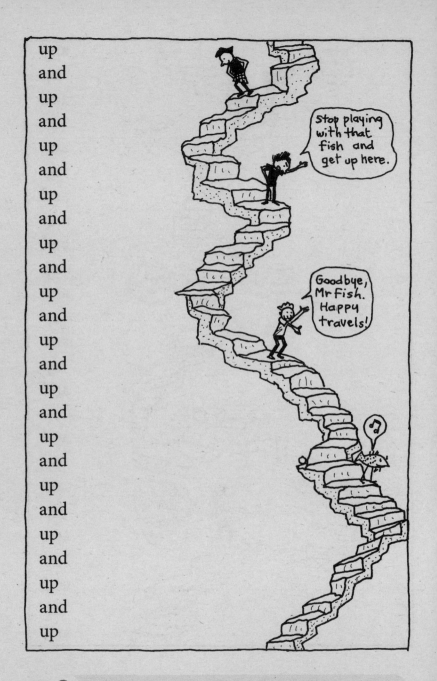

is red and the cat is red and the canary is red

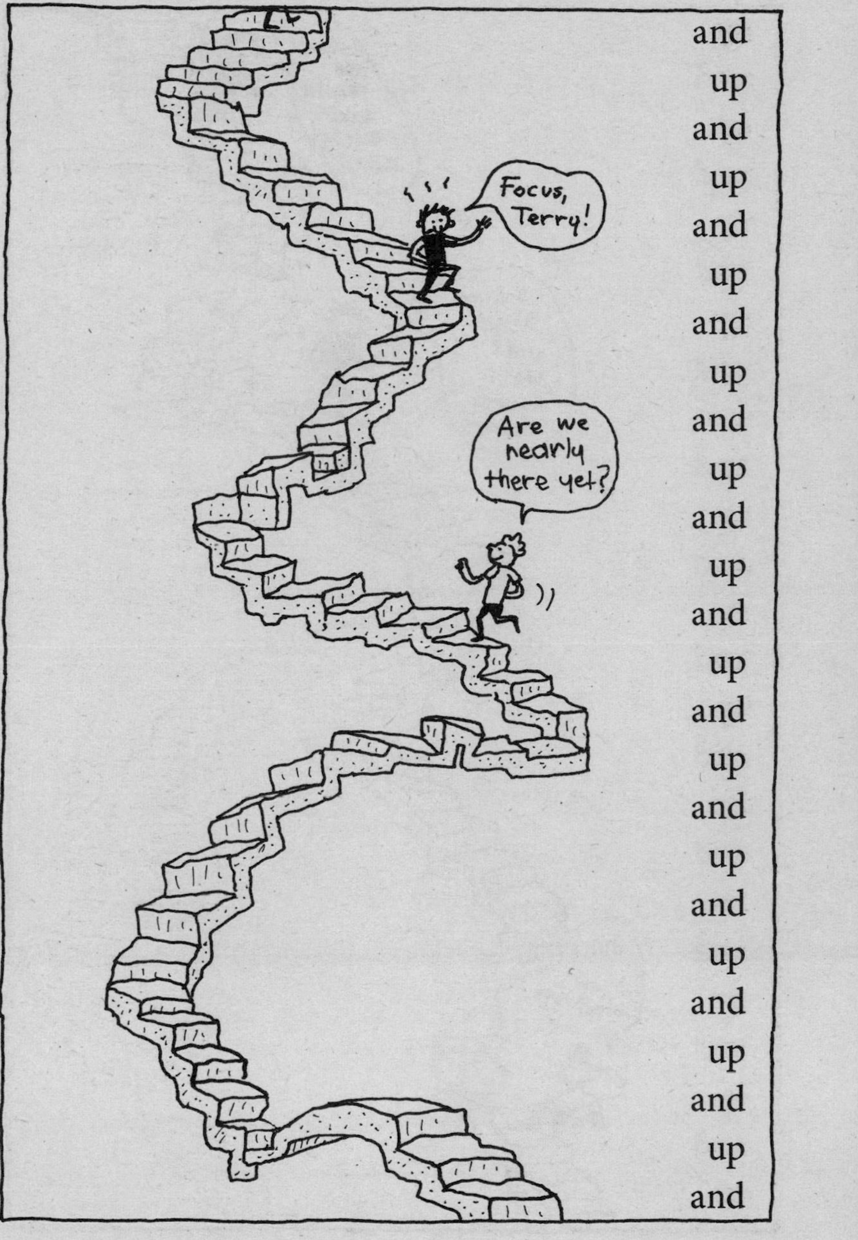
Focus, Terry!
Are we nearly there yet?

and
up
and
up
and
up
and
up
and
up
and
up
and
up
and
up
and
up
and
up
and
up
and
up
and

the fish tank are red. What colour are the stairs?

CHAPTER 8

PEEP! PEEP! PEEP!

'Are we there yet?' says Terry (for about the 50 millionth time).

'Almost,' I say. 'Just a few more steps.'

'Look,' says Jill. 'There's the nest!'

'Can you see my tooth?' I say.

'No,' says Jill. 'Just a bunch of the cutest baby birds I've ever seen!'

A   There are no stairs because it's a one-storey house!   199

We climb up a few more thousand steps until we are right across from the nest. But there's a big gap between the staircase and the nest. And a *long* drop back down to the ground.

'How are we going to get across?' says Terry. 'It's much too far to jump.'

'I know,' I say. 'It didn't look this far when we were looking up at it from the forest.'

'What about your emergency inflatable underpants, Terry?' says Jill. 'We could whoosh across in those.'

'I'm not wearing them,' he says. 'They got a puncture when we used them to sail to the desert island in the last book. But I *am* wearing my emergency inflatable ears.'

'Are you kidding me?' I say. 'Emergency inflatable *ears*?! That's the dumbest thing you've come up with since the Ninja Snail Training Academy.'

'Yeah, but my Ninja Snails saved the day,' says Terry, 'just like my emergency inflatable ears will. Watch this!'

He takes a deep breath, concentrates hard and then …

his ears inflate to about a thousand times their normal size!

'See?' he says. 'I told you!'

'You look so cute with big ears,' says Jill. 'Just like Dumbo the flying elephant!'

'Yeah, he looks dumb all right,' I say. 'But what use are they?'

'Well,' says Terry, 'they're flappable and really good for getting from, say, the steps of a never-ending staircase across to, say, a bird's nest. Climb into my ear and I'll take us there right now. Everybody ready? *Ear* we go!'

Terry launches himself from the staircase and starts flapping his ears as fast as he can.

THE DAY TERRY TURNED INTO AN EARPLANE.

How do you tell if there is an elephant in your fridge?

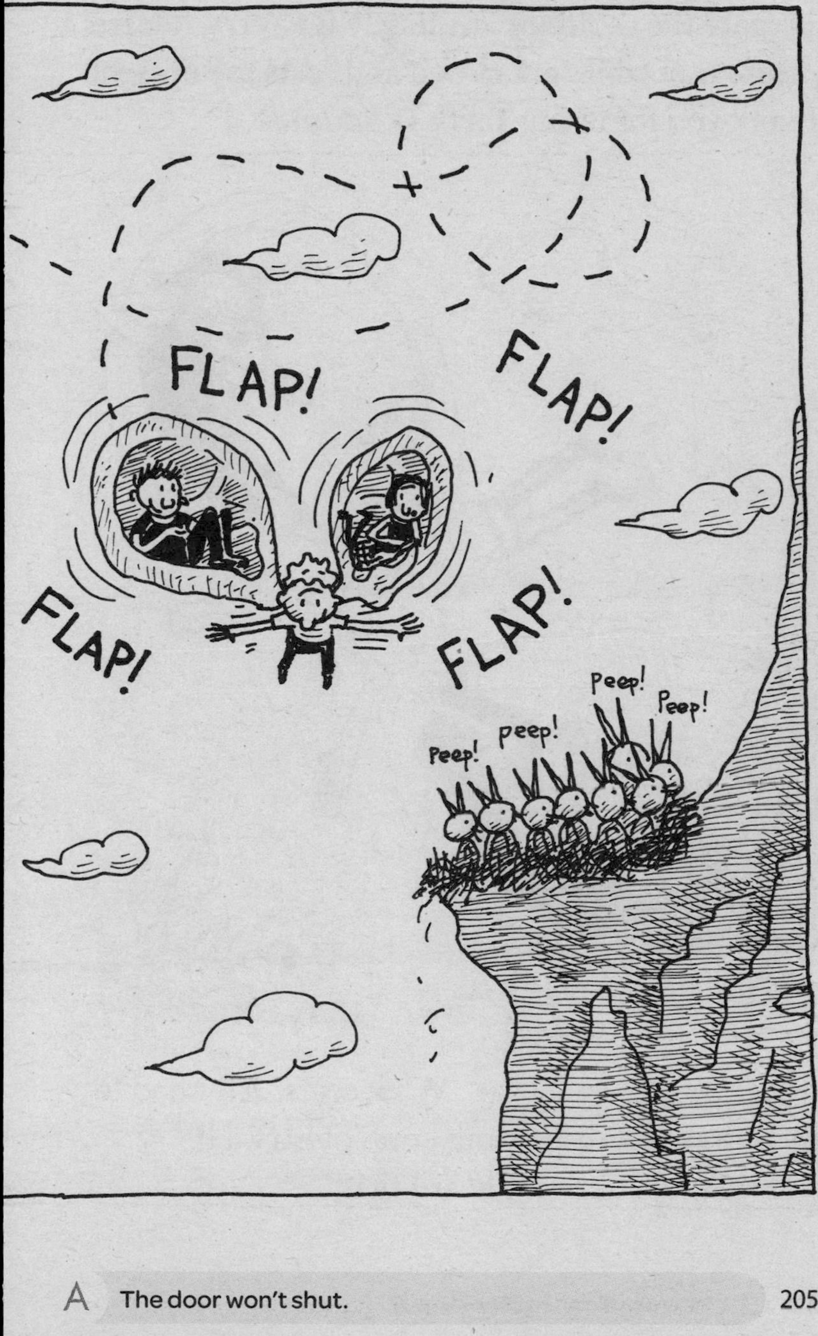
FLAP!
FLAP!
FLAP!
FLAP!
Peep!
peep!
Peep!
Peep!

'Prepare the cabin for landing,' says Terry. 'Please ensure tray tables are closed and seats are upright. Thank you for flying Terry D *Ear*lines.'

'What tray tables?' I say. 'What seats? All I had to sit on was this disgusting lump of earwax!'

'Hey!' says Terry. 'I heard that!'

Terry lands in the nest with a bump and Jill and I fall out of his ears.

We are immediately surrounded by a bunch of noisy baby birds, all pecking at us.

Terry's emergency inflatable ears don't stand a chance against the baby birds' sharp beaks.

'Hey, those baby birds just popped my ears!' says Terry.

'Yes, they're very pecky,' says Jill.

'I hate pecky birds,' I say. 'Let's look for my tooth and get out of here as fast as we can.'

'I think we may have to put off the tooth-hunt for the moment,' says Jill. 'Here comes the mother bird!'

'Eeek!' I say. 'Its beak looks even sharper and pointier than the baby birds' beaks. And much bigger!'

'Can you talk to it, Jill?' says Terry.

'Not while we're in her nest,' says Jill. 'If she sees us, she's going to peck first and ask questions later. Worm-snatchers are very protective of their young. We have to hide!'

'But there's nowhere *to* hide!' I say.

'In that case,' says Jill, 'we'll just have to pretend to be baby birds and hope she doesn't notice.'

We crouch down, put our hands on our hips and move our elbows back and forth.

'Cock-a-doodle-doo!' says Terry.

 If a rooster laid a brown egg and a white egg, what kind of chicks would hatch?

'You're supposed to be pretending to be a baby *worm-snatcher*, Terry,' says Jill. 'Not a rooster!'

'Oops,' says Terry. 'How about this: *Peep! Peep! Peep!*'

'Much better!' says Jill. 'I mean, *Peep! Peep! Peep!*'

The mother worm-snatcher lands, gripping the side of the nest with her enormous talons. Her beak is full of wriggling, writhing worms.

The *peep-peep-peeping* of the baby worm-snatchers is deafening. They all crane their necks to the sky and open their beaks wide. We do the same (except we have mouths, not beaks).

The mother worm-snatcher opens her beak and fresh, wriggling worms come raining down into our open mouths.

What do you get if you cross a worm and an elephant?

Erk! My mouth is full of cold, dirty, wriggling worms! Yuck! I'm trying not to chew or swallow them but it's not easy. It's like they *want* to wriggle down my throat.

But, weirdly, Terry doesn't seem to mind them at all. He's slurping them up like he's eating spaghetti!

At last, the mother bird runs out of worms, flaps her enormous wings and flies away.

'Yuck!' I say, spitting out the worms as fast as I can.

Q What did the worm say to the other worm when he was late home?

'Double yuck!' says Jill, spitting hers out too.
'No offence to worms.'

Terry doesn't spit his out, though. His mouth
is still full—so full, in fact, that there's a worm
hanging out of it.

One of the baby worm-snatchers snatches the end
of the worm and starts pulling on it.

Terry pulls back.

The bird pulls harder.

Terry pulls harder.

'Look at this, Jill,' I say. 'Terry is having a tug of worm with a baby bird.'

'Oh, come on, Terry,' says Jill. 'Let the baby bird have the worm.'

'But it's *my* worm,' Terry mumbles through a mouthful of worms. 'Mother gave it to *me*!'

While Terry is talking, the baby bird seizes its chance and snatches the worm and swallows it in one greedy gulp.

'Hey!' says Terry. 'That's not fair!'

'Yes, it is,' says Jill, 'because you're not *really* a baby bird and that mother bird was not *really* your mother.'

'I know,' sighs Terry. 'But I am *really* hungry.'

'So am I!' I say. 'But it doesn't change the fact that worms taste awful. I mean, that baby worm-snatcher over there is being sick. Not even worm-snatchers like worms!'

'It's not being *sick*,' says Jill. 'It's *choking*! It must have tried to eat too many worms at once. Stand back, I'm going to perform the *Wormlich* manoeuvre!'

GASP!

Jill picks up the bird, holds it upside down and squeezes it gently.

The bird coughs up a bunch of worms, including one with a really big white head and an extremely thin body. In fact, it doesn't look so much like a worm as a piece of string. A piece of string that is attached to …

MY TOOTH!

'I found my tooth!' I say.

'That must be what it was choking on,' says Jill.

'Yay!' says Terry. 'Now all our problems are solved.'

'Well, not all of them,' I say. 'We're still stuck in a nest on the top of Mount Everest with no way of getting down.'

'Oh, yeah,' says Terry. 'But hang on ... worms are really stretchy. When the mother bird comes back with another load of worms, we could tie them all together and make a worm-bungee to lower us safely back down to the ground.'

'We can't do that!' says Jill. 'That's cruelty to worms!'

'Maybe,' says Terry, 'but we'd be saving them from being eaten by birds, so we'd sort of be doing them a favour.'

'No, we wouldn't,' says Jill. 'Birds eating worms is nature's way; tying worms together to make a worm-bungee is not.'

At that moment we hear the sound of flapping wings and a mighty RAWK. We all turn around. The mother worm-snatcher is back—and she's seen us!

She dips her head down and swoops towards us.

'So long, Andy and Jill!' says Terry. 'It's been nice knowing you.'

'You too,' says Jill. 'And you too, Andy.'

But before I can reply, the baby bird that Jill saved flutters in between us and the mother bird. It *peep-peep-peeps* loudly and quickly.

'What's happening, Jill?' says Terry. 'What's the baby bird saying?'

'It's telling its mother how we saved it from choking,' says Jill.

The mother bird turns to us. 'RAWK! RAWK! RAWK!' she rawks.

'What does that mean, Jill?' I say. 'Is it good or bad?'

'It's good,' says Jill. '*Very* good. She says she is extremely grateful and that if there's ever anything she can do to repay us for our quick-thinking and kindness, we only have to ask.'

What do you get if you cross a parrot with a shark?

'Do you think she could give us a lift back down to the treehouse?' I say.

'I'll ask her,' says Jill. She turns to the mother bird. 'Rawk rawk rawk?'

RAWK, RAWK, RAWK. RAWK.

The mother bird rawks back at her.

'She says yes, she'd be happy to,' says Jill.

We climb up onto the mother bird's back. The feathers are hard and slippery and very difficult to hold on to.

'We can use the string as a set of reins,' says Jill, throwing it around the bird's neck. 'Everybody ready? Let's fly!'

The worm-snatcher flaps her wings, alights from the nest and begins a rapid descent.

Down
and
down
and
down
we
fly.

Down
and
down
and
down
and
down
and
down
and
down
and
down
and
down
and
down
and
down
and
down
and
down
and
down
and
down
and
down
and
down

Q What is the most uncomfortable of all birds?

and
down
and
down
and
down
and
down
and
down
and
down
and
down
and
down
and
down
and
down
and
down
and
down
and
down
and
down
and

down
and
down
and
down
and
down
and
down
and
down
and
down
and
down
and
down
and
down
and
down
and
down
and
down
and
down
and
down

Which bird is always out of breath?

and
down
and
down
and
down
and
down
and
down
and
down
and
down
and
down
and
down
and
down
and
down
and
down
and
down
and
down
and

A A puffin.

down
and
down
and
down
and
down
and
down
and
down
and
down
and
down
and
down
and
down
and
down
and
down
and
down
and
down
and
down

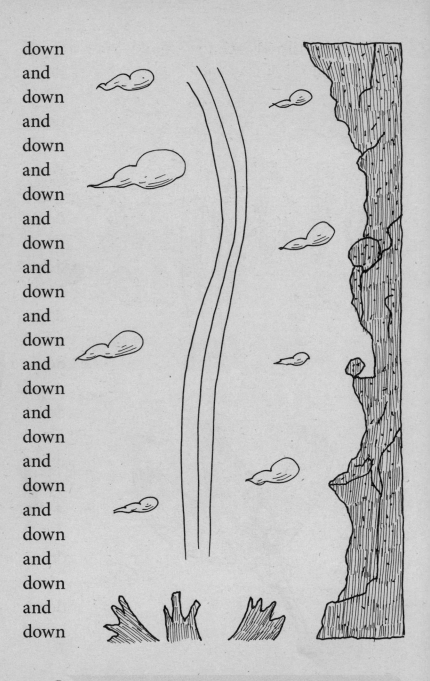

Q What is a bird's favourite part of the TV news?

and down until we reach the ground. We climb off
the bird and Jill thanks her.

They have a long rawking conversation and then
the bird rawks gratefully at us one last time and
takes off again.

'What were you and the bird rawking about?' I say.

'She said that if we ever needed her help again, all we have to do is rawk,' says Jill. 'What a big adventure we've had! I'm going to go straight home and tell my animals all about it.'

Why did the bird bring toilet paper to the party?

CHAPTER 9

TERRY, WILL YOU PLEASE BE QUIET, PLEASE?

'Well, I sure am glad that's over,' I say. 'Now I've got my tooth back I'm going to go to bed right away so the tooth fairy can come and give me two dollars!'

A   Because it was a party-pooper.   237

'But it's *way* too early to go to bed,' says Terry. 'It's still daytime.'

'I know,' I say, 'but I can't wait until tonight—we have to get our book done before then. So can you please be *really* quiet so I can get to sleep?'

Why does a dragon sleep all day?

'Sure thing, Andy,' says Terry. 'You can count on me! Goodnight!'

'Goodnight, Terry,' I say.

I climb the ladder to my bedroom, put on my pyjamas and get into bed.

I am actually feeling quite tired after climbing the never-ending staircase so I don't think it's going to be too difficult to fall asleep. In fact, I'm falling asleep right now.

I'm falling ...

falling ...

falling ...

Q What question can you never answer yes to?

falling ...

falling ...

falling ...

CLOMP!

I'm almost asleep when I hear really loud
clomping. It's so loud my bed is shaking.

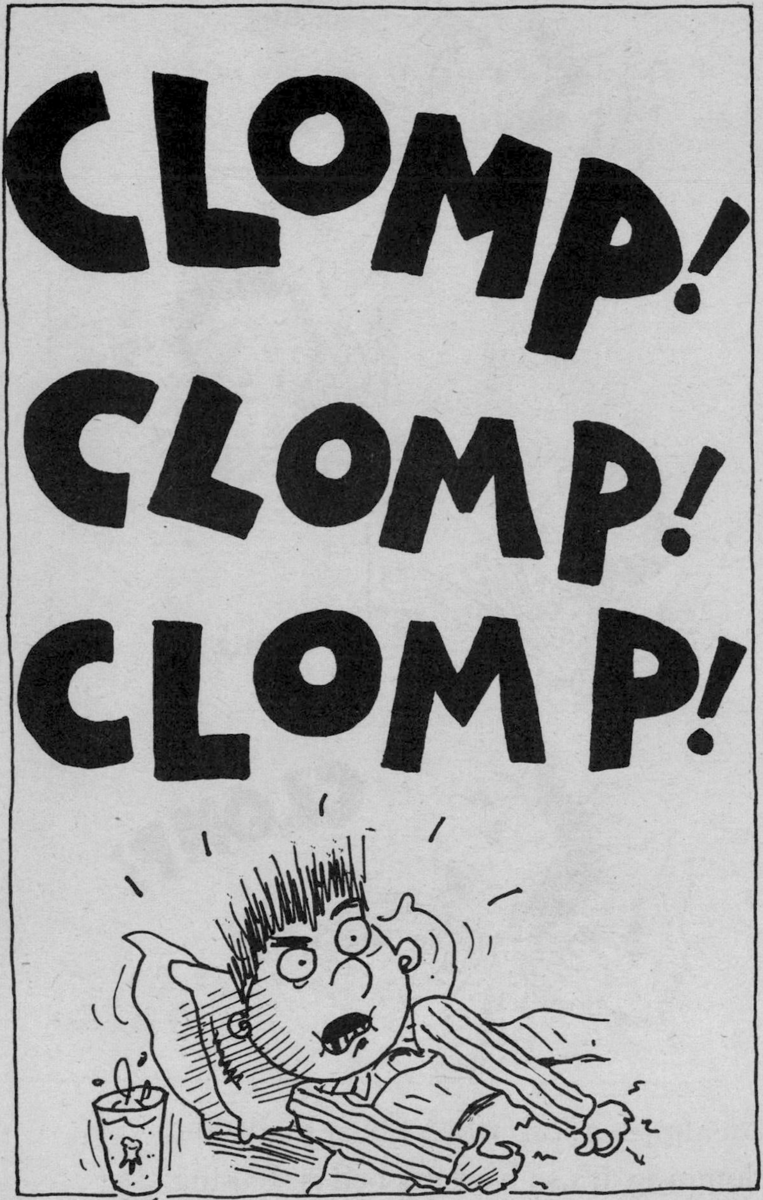
CLOMP!
CLOMP!
CLOMP!

I get out of bed, look over the edge and see Terry clomping around in a gigantic pair of clomping boots!

'Hey, Terry,' I yell. 'Quit clomping, will you? I'm trying to get to sleep!'

'Sorry, Andy!' he says. 'I was just testing these new, extra-loud clomping boots I invented. Turns out they're even louder than I expected. But I'll take them off now. I won't disturb you again, I promise.'

'You'd better not!' I say. 'GOODNIGHT!'

'Goodnight, Andy,' says Terry.

I go back to bed and try to fall asleep again.

I'm falling …

falling …

falling …

falling …

falling …

falling …

GRANGLE!

I'm almost asleep when I hear some of the loudest—
and most ridiculous—noises I've ever heard.

PARRP! BLEEK! SPROING!

Q   How do you get a baby astronaut to sleep?

I get out of bed, look over the edge and see Terry wearing an extra-stupid, super-loud hat!

'Terry!' I yell, but he can't hear me over the deafening noise of his stupid hat.

'TERRY!' I yell again, even louder.

But he still can't hear me.
'TERRY!' I yell as loud as I can.

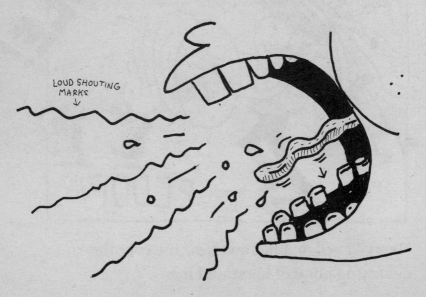

This time he hears me.

'Sorry, Andy,' he says. 'I couldn't hear you over the noise of this extra-stupid, super-loud hat. What's the matter?'

'Your extra-stupid, super-loud hat is the matter!' I say. 'I'm trying to get to sleep, remember?'

'Oh, sorry, Andy,' says Terry. 'I forgot. I'll take it off and be very, very quiet from now on. I promise.'

'You'd better be,' I say. 'OR ELSE!'

I go back to bed and start falling asleep for the third time.

I'm falling …

falling …

falling …

falling …

falling …

Why did the girl tiptoe past the medicine cabinet?

falling ...

falling ...

falling ...

falling ...

I get out of bed, look over the edge and see Terry playing drums, Superfinger playing guitar, and the Trunkinator dancing in an extra-large pair of extra-loud clomping boots …

What's the best present you can receive for Christmas?

and to make it even worse, they're all wearing extra-stupid, super-loud hats!

Right! That does it! I take a deep breath and yell ...

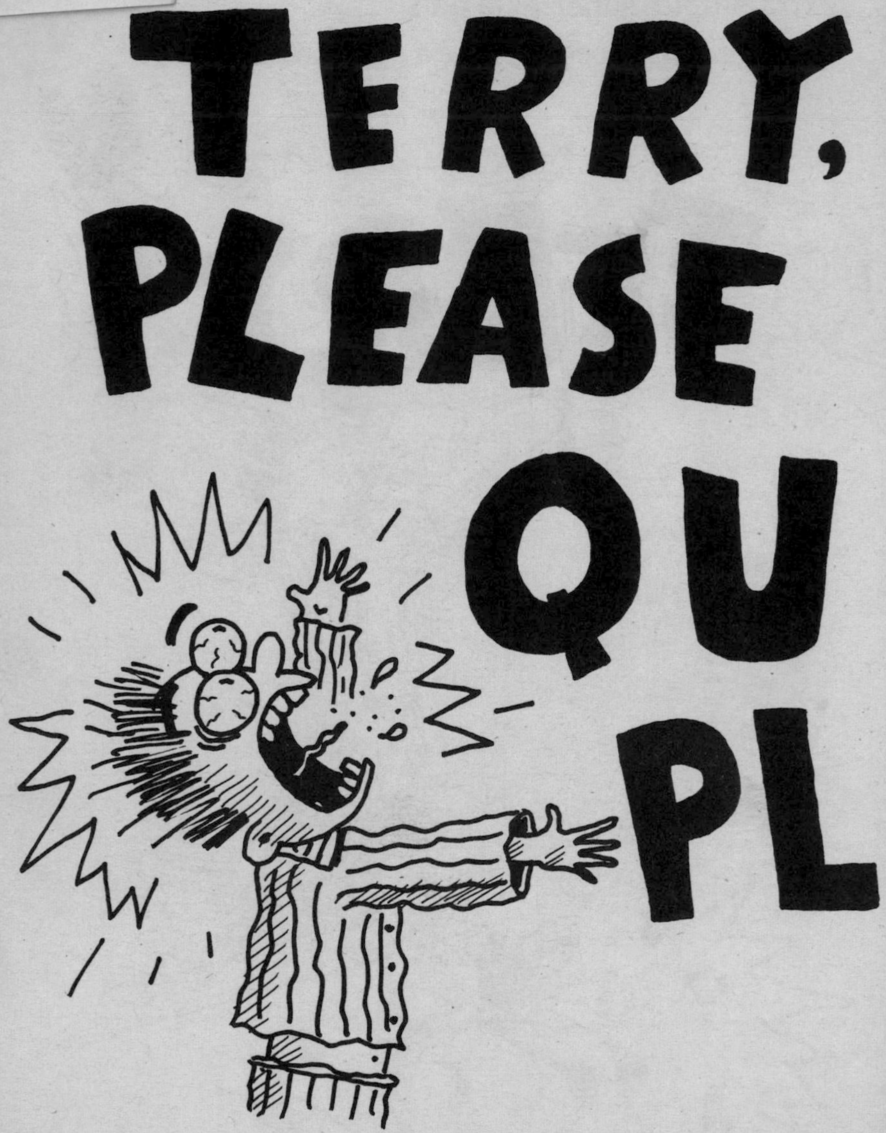
TERRY,
PLEASE
QU
PL

 Q What breaks every time you name it?

WILL YOU BE IET, EASE?!

'Sorry, Andy,' says Terry. 'We were just practising our act for the Treehouse Talent Quest.'

'What Treehouse Talent Quest?' I say.

'The one I thought we could have after this book is finished.'

'This book won't *be* finished,' I say, 'if you don't let me get to sleep!!!'

Did you hear about the soldier who bought a camouflage sleeping bag?

'I'll be quiet now,' says Terry. 'I promise.'

'That's what you said last time!' I say.

'I know,' says Terry, 'but it won't happen again, I really promise. I'll be as quiet as a mouse.'

'All right,' I say. 'Goodnight … *for the last time*!'

I go back to bed and start falling asleep …

falling …

falling …

falling …

asleep.

Q Why couldn't Dracula's wife go to sleep?

CHAPTER 10

TERRY AND THE TOOTH FAIRY

'Twas the day of the toothache, when all
   through the tree
Not a creature was stirring—no, not even me.
Andy's tooth had been placed
In a small glass with care
In the hopes that the tooth fairy soon would
   be there.

A   Because of his coffin.

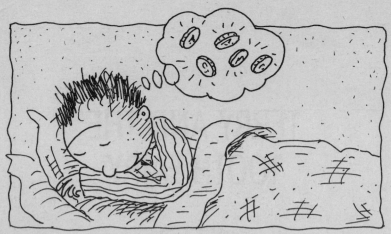

 Andy was nestled all snug in his bed,
While visions of gold coins danced in his head.

 And me in the bathtub, blowing a bubble.
Trying my hardest to stay out of trouble.*

*And be really, really quiet!

What TV program should you watch in the bath?

When out in the forest there arose
   such a clatter,
I sprang from my bath to see what
   was the matter.
A towel wrapped around me, I flew
   like a breeze,
To the edge of the decking and peered
   through the leaves.

And what to my wondering eyes should appear,
But a little steam-powered machine
   drawing near.
And a tiny toy truck with a miniature crane,
From which dangled a hook on a small
   golden chain.

All led by a figure, so lively and airy,
I knew in a moment it must be the tooth fairy!
More rapid than eagles to the treehouse
    she came,
And she whistled, and shouted, and called her
    helpers by name!

A A garbage truck.

'Come, Achey! Come, Molar! Come, Driller!
   Come, Smash!
To the top of the tree! To the bedroom
   let's dash!
And we'll heave away, haul away our
   pearly prize
For it's teeth that we gather, no matter
   the size!'

What is the best thing to put into pies?

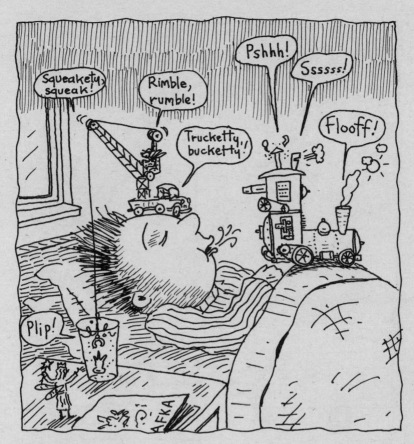

And up through the treehouse the
    tiny crew flew,
With both their machines and the
    tooth fairy too.
They parked their small truck on
    Andy's sweet head
And lowered the hook to the glass by his bed.

A   Your teeth.

And then with a chant of 'Tooth-heave' and
   'Tooth-ho',
The tooth was brought up from the water below.
It was placed in the truck and tied up
   very tightly.
With gossamer ropes that glistened
   quite brightly.

Q   What has teeth but cannot eat?

The tooth fairy flittered and fluttered
    with glee.
'Pay him,' she said, 'his tooth fairy fee.'
The machine began whirring.
It whistled and blew.
And then out of a slot a two-dollar coin flew.

A   A comb.

Up through the air flew the newly made cash,
Then into the glass it fell with a splash.
'And now,' said the fairy, 'it's home we
    must dash
To deliver this tooth for the queen's
    birthday bash!'

What game do cats play at birthday parties?

She sprang to the truck,
To her team gave a whistle,
And away they all flew like the down
    of a thistle.
But I heard her exclaim, as she drove
    out of sight,
'Thanks for the tooth, and to all a goodnight.'

A Mew-sical chairs.

I decided to follow, for to tell you the truth,
I wanted to see what they'd do with the tooth.
Across land, sea and rivers the fairy
   crew flew
And not far behind them, I also flew too.

For hours and hours, **I** followed that band
Until, finally, we reached it—the
    famed Fairyland!
The lights of the city were sparkling
    and shining
And fairies galore were all dancing and dining.

A   Time.   271

The city was holding a great celebration,
A big birthday treat for the queen of
    their nation.
Andy's tooth was unloaded by the fairies
    with care,
Put into a cannon and shot into the air.

And though not a good tooth—it was
   badly corroded—
Andy's molar looked great as it BOOMED
   and exploded!
(Who would have thought that a tooth
   with decay
Could produce such a wonderful
   fireworks display?)

A   They shell-ebrate.

THE NIGHT ANDY'S TOOTH WAS SHOT OUT OF A CANNON IN FAIRY LAND

Q What do you get when you cross a dinosaur with fireworks?

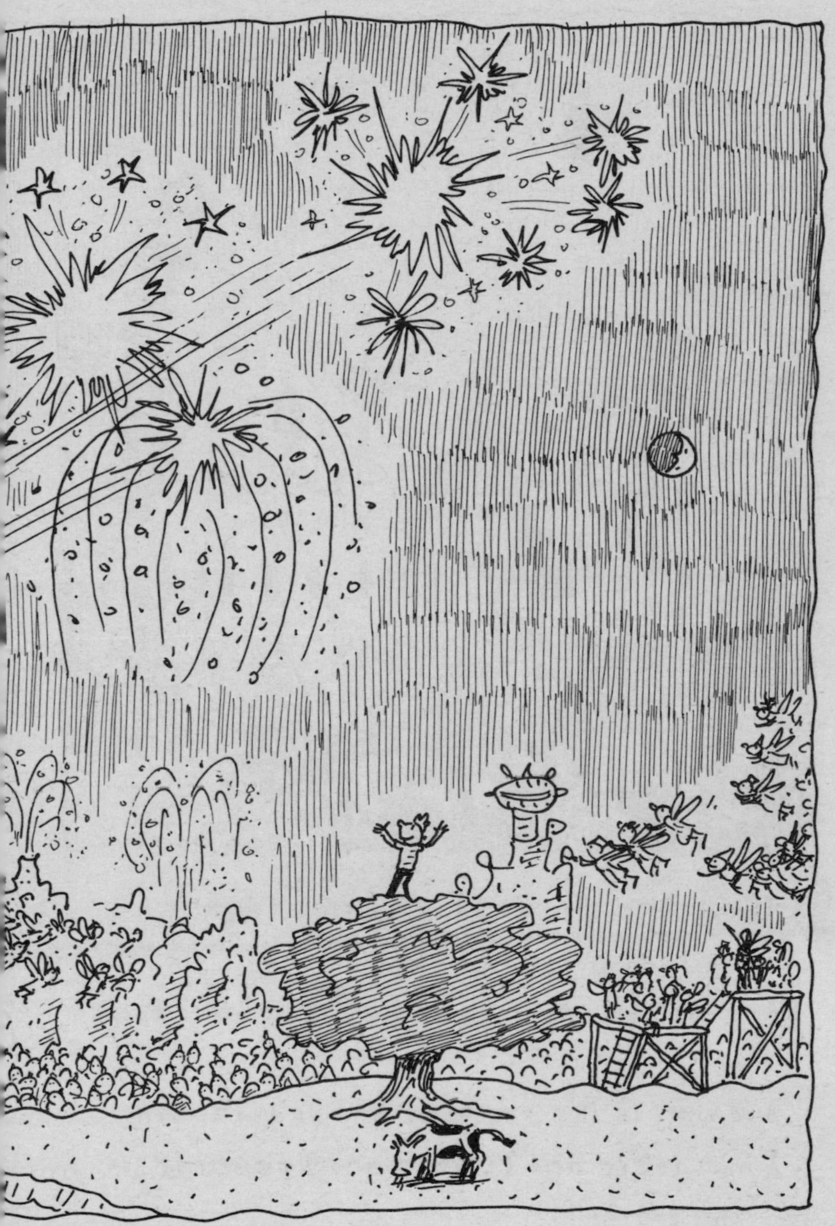

The queen thanked the fairies for her
   birthday surprise
And for the amazing display that had dazzled
   her eyes.
And that is the story of Andy's old tooth.
I was there and **I** saw it and **I** swear it's
   the truth!

What did one eye say to the other eye?

CHAPTER 11

LET'S GO SHOPPING!

'There's something between us that smells.'

'Wake up, Andy!' says Terry, shaking me roughly. 'Andy! Wake up!'

'What is it *now*, Terry?' I say. 'You promised to be *quiet*! I'm trying to get to sleep so the tooth fairy can come!'

'You *did* fall asleep!' says Terry. 'And the tooth fairy *did* come!'

'Really?' I say.

    'Yes,' says Terry, picking up the glass. 'Look!'

At the bottom of the glass is a shiny, brand-new two-dollar coin.

'It worked!' I say. 'We've got the two dollars we need. But how did you know?'

'I saw the whole thing!' says Terry. 'They made so much noise I was afraid they were going to wake you up.'

'They?' I say. 'I thought there was only one tooth fairy.'

'There is,' says Terry, breathlessly, 'but she had a whole gang of helpers and they had a little truck with a crane and a money-making machine just like ours—only it was tiny, and it didn't make honey. I followed them back to Fairyland and I saw them use your tooth as a firework to help celebrate the fairy queen's birthday!'

A To prevent bat breath.

'Are you sure you didn't fall asleep as well?' I say. 'Sounds like you've been dreaming.'

'No, it's *true*,' says Terry. 'You can ask the readers. They were there too. They saw me see the whole thing!'

'It's not that I don't *believe* you,' I say. 'But I think I will check with them anyway.'

Well, readers, *is* it true? Did Terry really see all that stuff?

What is Dracula's favourite fruit?

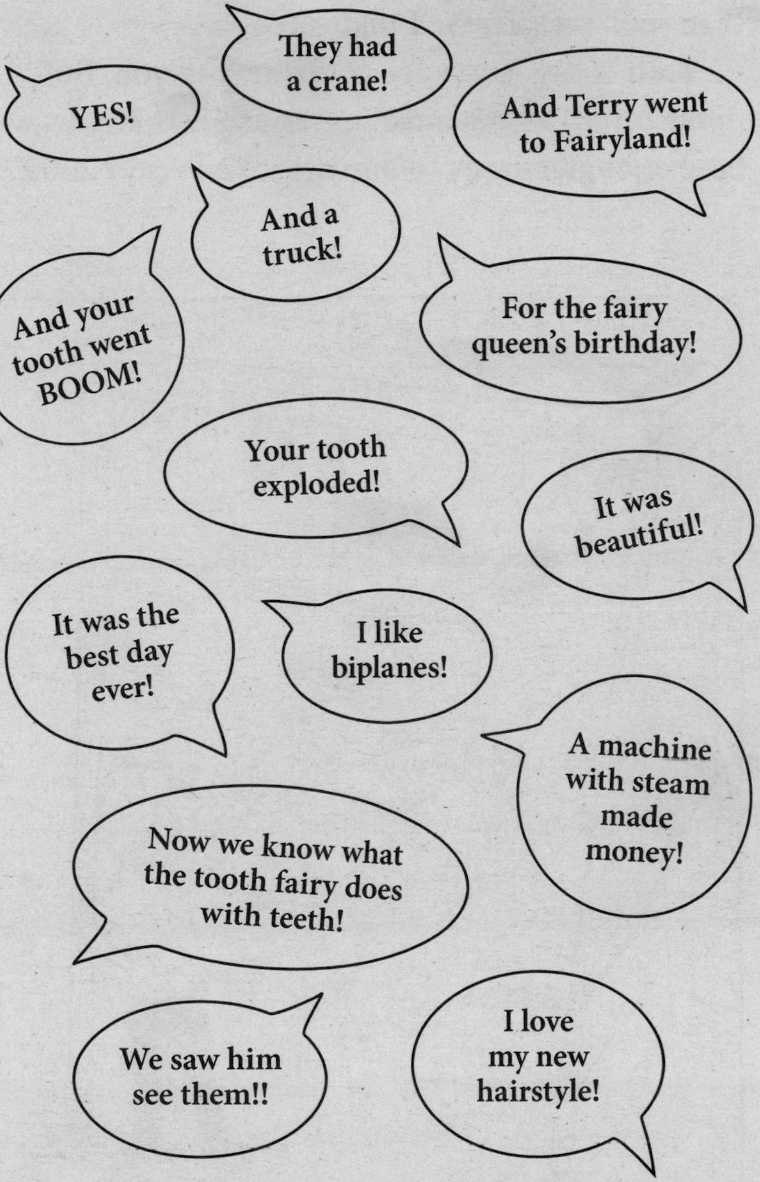
They had a crane!
YES!
And Terry went to Fairyland!
And a truck!
For the fairy queen's birthday!
And your tooth went BOOM!
Your tooth exploded!
It was beautiful!
It was the best day ever!
I like biplanes!
A machine with steam made money!
Now we know what the tooth fairy does with teeth!
We saw him see them!!
I love my new hairstyle!

'You see?' says Terry. 'I told you!'

'Yeah,' I say, 'sorry for not believing you. But never mind, what's most important is that now we have enough money to buy the Joke Writer 2000™!'

Where can you always find money?

I get out of bed and get dressed. We grab the rest of our money, jump onto our jet-propelled office chairs and fly as fast as we can to the Two-Million-Dollar Shop.

A In the dictionary.

'Ah, I was wondering when you'd be back,' says Fancy Fish.

'Do you still have the Joke Writer 2000™?' says Terry.

'Yes,' says Fancy Fish, 'but there's been a lot of interest since you left. You're *very* lucky it's still available.'

'We'll buy it!' I say.

'An excellent decision, sir,' says Fancy Fish. 'Would you like it gift-wrapped? I have some very fancy wrapping paper for only two million dollars: the finest-quality wrapping paper in the land—or in the sea!'

What kind of ant is really good at mathematics?

'No, thanks,' I say, 'it's not a gift; it's for us—we need it for our book.'

'As you please,' says Fancy Fish, putting his fin out. 'That will be four million dollars, please.'

'*Four* million dollars?' says Terry.

'Yes, that is correct,' says Fancy Fish.

'But it was only *two* million dollars before,' I say.

'I know,' says Fancy Fish, shrugging, 'but since then the price has gone up.'

'But this is the *Two*-Million-Dollar Shop,' I say.

'Exactly!' he says. 'Nothing *under* two million dollars. That's our promise to you.'

'But you can't just double the price of something for no reason,' says Terry.

'I think you'll find I can,' says Fancy Fish, pointing to a sign above the counter.

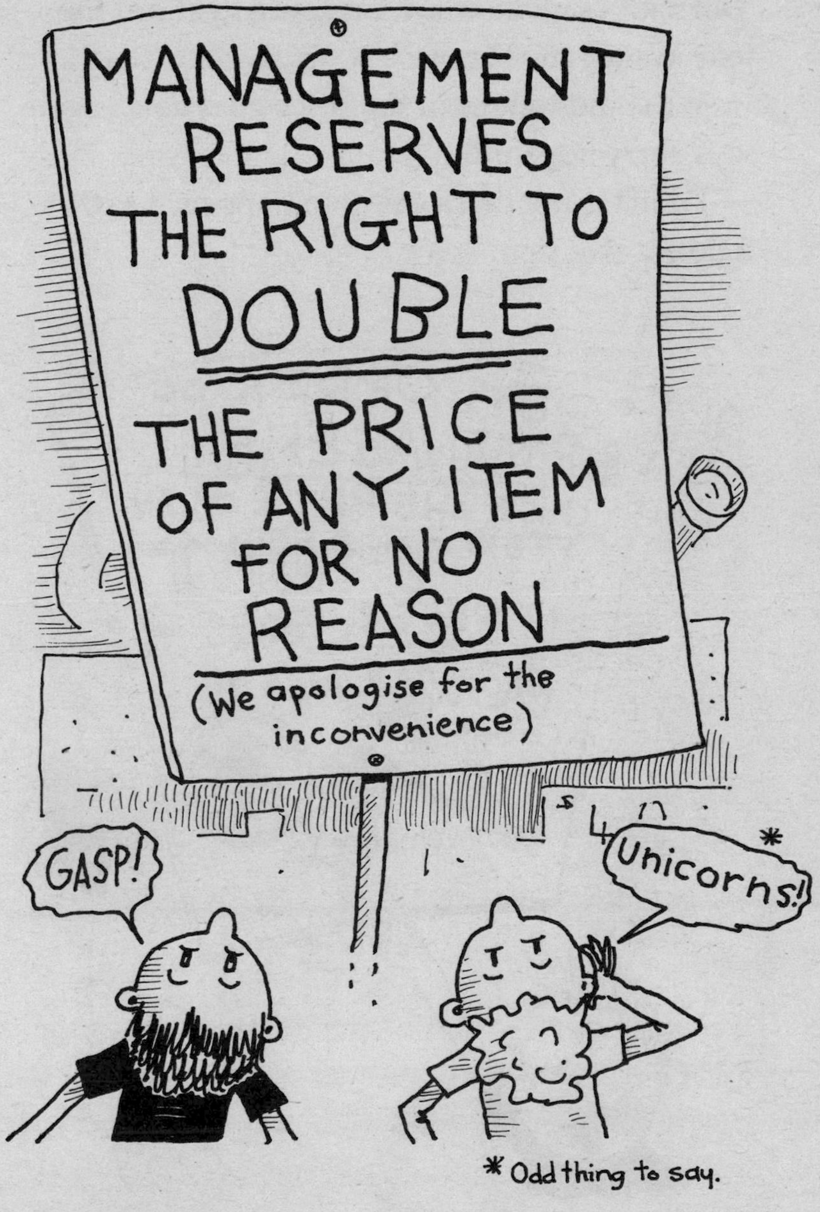
MANAGEMENT RESERVES THE RIGHT TO DOUBLE THE PRICE OF ANY ITEM FOR NO REASON
(We apologise for the inconvenience)
GASP!
Unicorns! *
* Odd thing to say.

A Put it in front of a mirror.

'Darn it!' I say. 'How are we going to afford the Joke Writer 2000™ now?'

'We could wait until the price goes *down* again,' says Terry hopefully.

'I don't think that's going to happen,' I say. 'Look at *that* sign.'

How much money does a skunk have?

'This shop is too expensive,' says Terry. 'I wish we'd never put it in our treehouse.'

'Me, too,' I say. 'But, on the other hand, it's the *only* shop where we can buy a Joke Writer 2000™ and we *need* a Joke Writer 2000™!'

'Yeah, I know,' says Terry. 'I guess we're just going to have to find *another* two million dollars. Maybe we could pull out some more of your teeth. The fairy queen was very happy with your last tooth. Perhaps the tooth fairy would pay us *more* than two dollars per tooth—especially if we explained the situation.'

'No way!' I say. 'You are not pulling out any more of my teeth! Besides, I've got a *much* better idea.'

'What is it?' says Terry.

'We can go to the Two-Dollar Shop and use my new two-dollar coin to buy another two million dollars. Then we'll have *four* million dollars and we can come back and buy the Joke Writer 2000™!'

'Wow,' says Terry, 'you are getting *much* better at maths, Andy! But you've made a slight miscalculation. If we use your two dollars to buy two *million* dollars, we'll still be two dollars short, so we need to buy two million and *two* dollars.'

'Oh, yeah,' I say.

I turn to Fancy Fish. 'Hold that Joke Writer 2000™! We'll be right back!'

We rush to the Two-Dollar Shop. When we arrive Pinchy McPhee is out the front beside a big pile of money and a MONEY SALE sign.

If there are four dollars and you take away three, how many do you have?

'We're in luck, Andy!' says Terry. 'Pinchy is having a money sale! All the money is only two dollars! This is the *best* value shop in the whole treehouse!'

'You're right about that!' says Pinchy. 'How can I help you?'

'We'd like to buy two million and two dollars, please,' I say.

'Certainly,' says Pinchy. He grabs a big pile of cash and puts it on the counter.

'There you go,' he says. 'Two million and two dollars! That will be two dollars, please. Would you like that gift-wrapped?'

'No, thanks,' I say, 'it's not a gift; it's for us—we need it to buy a Joke Writer 2000™ for our book.'

I hand over my new two-dollar coin. 'Thanks, Pinchy!'

'Thank *you*,' says Pinchy, pinching the shiny gold coin in his pincer. 'I think I feel a song coming on!'

'Uh-oh,' whispers Terry. 'Let's get out of here!'

A Baby giraffes.

When we get back to the Two-Million-Dollar Shop Fancy Fish is waiting for us, still holding the Joke Writer 2000™ in his fin.

'Well?' he says. 'What's your decision?'

'We'll buy it!' I say.

'Wonderful,' says Fancy Fish. 'That will be eight million dollars, please!'

'WHAT?!' I say. '*EIGHT* MILLION DOLLARS?!'

'YOU CAN'T DOUBLE THE PRICE AGAIN!' says Terry. 'IT'S NOT RIGHT AND IT'S NOT *FAIR!*'

'Relax,' says Fancy Fish. 'Keep your scales on! I was just having a little joke. The price is still four million dollars.'

'Phew!' says Terry, as we dump the money on the counter. 'For a moment there I thought we were going to have to go back to the Two-Dollar Shop and buy even *more* money!'

Fancy Fish sweeps all the money off the counter with a swift swish of his fancy fins and then puts the Joke Writer 2000™ in my hand. I immediately feel 110 per cent funnier. This book is going to be good. This book is going to be great. This book is going to be the goodest, greatest, funniest book we have ever written!

What do you get when you cross a fish and a kitten?

CHAPTER 12

JOKE-WRITING TIME

Before we can start work, however, we really need to eat. After all that stair-climbing and sleeping and shopping both Terry and I are feeling pretty hungry.

The marshmallow machine senses our hunger and starts firing marshmallows into our mouths at high speed.

Why did the elephant stand on the marshmallow?

'I'm full!' I say.

'Me, too,' says Terry.

We close our mouths and the marshmallow machine fires marshmallows at our faces for a while and then drifts away to see if anybody else in the treehouse is hungry.

'Right,' I say. '*Now* we can get started.'

I pick up the Joke Writer 2000™. It's surprisingly heavy and for a moment I wonder how I'm actually going to write with it, but then something incredible happens—it leaps out of my hand and starts writing all by itself!

'Look, Terry!' I say. 'It's writing automatically! I'm not doing *anything*!'

'Wow!' says Terry. 'That's amazing! It's doing all the work. I can't wait to see why the koala fell out of the tree. I bet it will be hilarious.'

'Well, you won't have to wait long,' I say. 'It's writing the answer right now!'

'I was right,' says Terry. 'It *is* hilarious! Make it write another one.'

I put the tip of the Joke Writer 2000™ on the paper and it starts writing again.

What do you get if you cross a lemon and a cat?

'That's even funnier than the first one,' says Terry.

'I know!' I say. 'This pencil is fantastic!'

'Can I have a go?' says Terry.

'Sure,' I say, passing it to him.

Terry puts the tip of the pencil on the paper. It breaks free of his grip and takes off again.

Terry laughs so hard he snorts milk out of his nose—and he's not even drinking milk!

'Oh, boy,' says Terry. 'This pencil is amazing!'

'I know,' I say. 'With a pencil *this* funny, we'll be able to write the funniest books ever!'

'The Joke Writer 2000™ is worth every single dollar we paid for it,' says Terry.

'It sure is,' I say. 'It's worth every bun that knocked us backwards, every flying fridge that almost flattened us, every single stair we climbed on the never-ending staircase and every slimy, revolting, wriggling worm we ate in the worm-snatcher's nest. It's the greatest pencil ever!'

As we stand there admiring the Joke Writer 2000™, we see a bird flying towards us.

'Hey, that looks like the worm-snatcher,' says Terry.

'Sort of,' I say, 'but it's the wrong colour.'

Suddenly the bird dives at great speed, snatches
the Joke Writer 2000™ out of Terry's hand and
takes off, back up into the sky.

'Oh, no,' says Terry, 'not again!'

We are just standing there—stunned—when Jill pokes her head and shoulders up through the branches, her binoculars around her neck.

'Did you just see a high-flying, mountain-dwelling Joke Writer-snatcher come through here?' she says. 'I lost track of it when it dived into the treehouse.'

'We saw it all right!' I say. 'It just swooped down here and snatched our Joke Writer 2000™!'

'They do that,' says Jill. 'That's why they're called Joke Writer-snatchers.'

'Don't tell me we have to climb the never-ending staircase up to Mount Everest *again*,' says Terry.

'No,' I say. 'Actually, I don't think we do. And you know what? I'm not sure that we needed to climb it in the first place.'

'Yes, we did,' says Terry. 'We needed to get your tooth.'

'I know we *thought* we did,' I say, 'but I've just realised that after you pulled my tooth out back in chapter six I haven't had any toothache so I don't really need the Joke Writer 2000™ to help me write.'

Terry frowns. 'So if we didn't need to climb the never-ending staircase to get your tooth,' he says, 'does that mean we didn't need to pretend to be baby birds and eat all those worms?'

'Well, you didn't have to eat quite so *many* worms,' I say. 'But, no, we didn't need to do that either.'

'And I didn't need to be really quiet so you could go to sleep and the tooth fairy would come?'

'No,' I say.

'That means I had a bath for nothing!' says Terry. 'And we spent *four million dollars* on a joke-writing pencil that we only got three jokes out of. We could have bought the solid gold toilet seat after all! And now we don't have any money left!'

'I know,' I say, 'but it is *kind* of funny when you think about it.'

Terry thinks about it. And then he thinks about it some more. He frowns—and then he laughs. 'You're right,' he says. 'It *is* pretty funny that we did all that stuff we didn't even need to do.'

Jill laughs, too. 'And look on the bright side,' she says. 'It's going to make a great story for your book.'

'Yeah!' says Terry. 'Especially now Andy's got his sense of humour back!'

'I sure have,' I say. 'I'm feeling funny enough to write the book *and* all the jokes … with your help, of course.'

'And mine!' says Jill. 'I know lots of *animal* jokes. Listen to this one: What do you call a sleeping dinosaur?'

'I don't know,' I say. 'What?'

'A dino-snore!' says Jill.

'That joke is not only funny, it's *true*!' says Terry. 'Let's get started right away!'

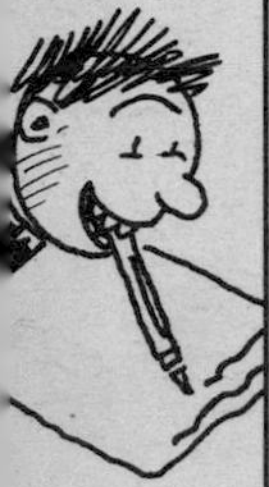

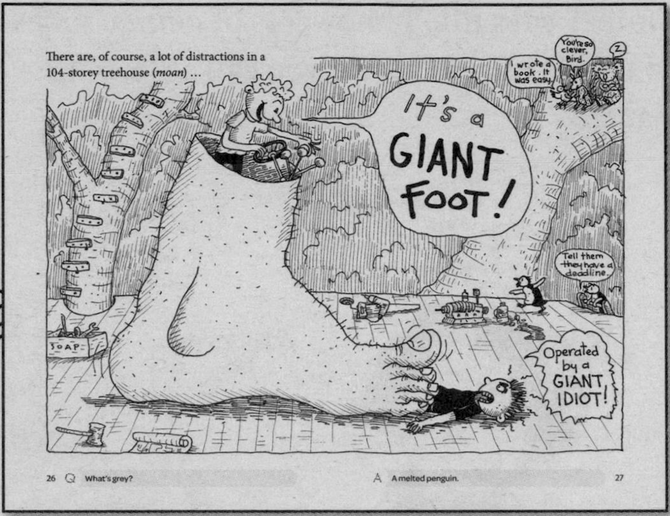
There are, of course, a lot of distractions in a 104-storey treehouse (*moan*) …

It's a GIANT FOOT!
You're so clever, Bird.
I wrote a book. It was easy.
Z
Tell them ~~they~~ have a deadline.
Operated by a GIANT IDIOT!
SOAP

26 Q What's grey?

A A melted penguin. 27

So we write …

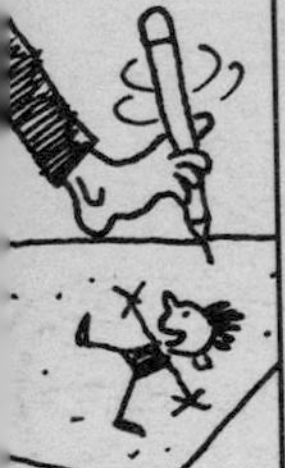

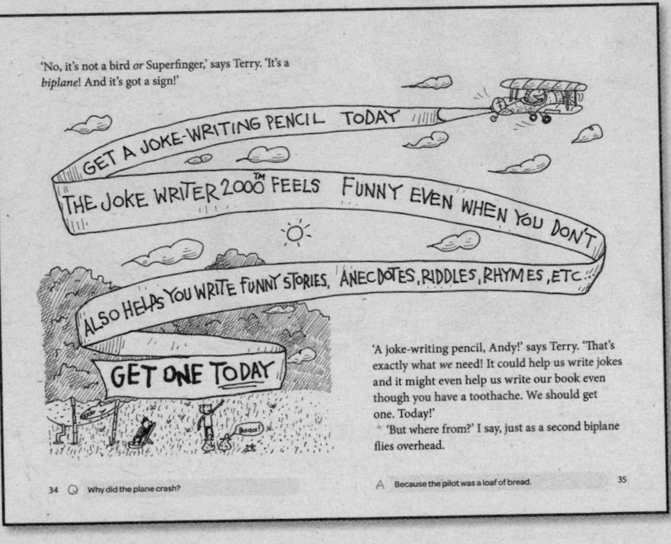
'No, it's not a bird *or* Superfinger,' says Terry. 'It's a *biplane*! And it's got a sign!'

GET A JOKE-WRITING PENCIL TODAY
THE JOKE WRITER 2000™ FEELS FUNNY EVEN WHEN YOU DON'T
ALSO HELPS YOU WRITE FUNNY STORIES, ANECDOTES, RIDDLES, RHYMES, ETC.
GET ONE TODAY

'A joke-writing pencil, Andy!' says Terry. 'That's exactly what *we* need! It could help us write jokes and it might even help us write our book even though you have a toothache. We should get one. Today!'

'But where from?' I say, just as a second biplane flies overhead.

34 Q Why did the plane crash?

A Because the pilot was a loaf of bread. 35

and we draw …

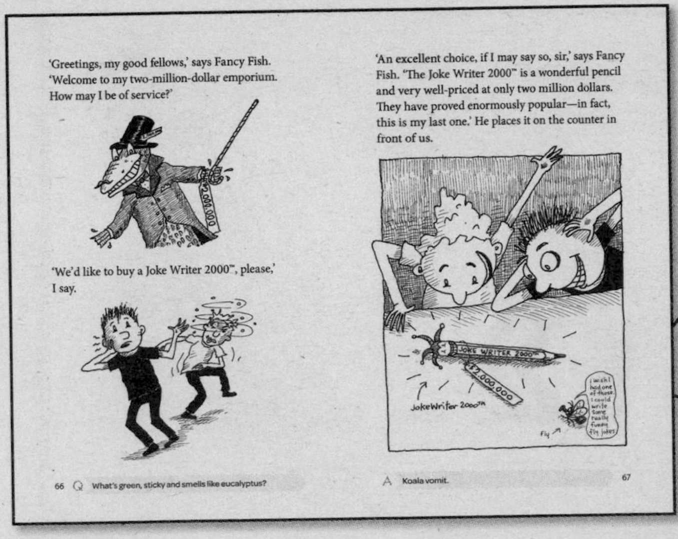
'Greetings, my good fellows,' says Fancy Fish. 'Welcome to my two-million-dollar emporium. How may I be of service?'

'We'd like to buy a Joke Writer 2000™, please,' I say.

'An excellent choice, if I may say so, sir,' says Fancy Fish. 'The Joke Writer 2000™ is a wonderful pencil and very well-priced at only two million dollars. They have proved enormously popular—in fact, this is my last one.' He places it on the counter in front of us.

JOKE WRITER 2000™
$2,000,000
JokeWriter 2000™
Fly

66 Q What's green, sticky and smells like eucalyptus?

A Koala vomit. 67

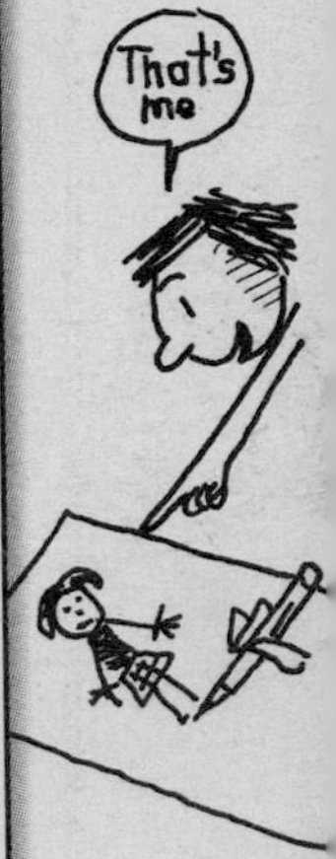

That's me

and we draw…

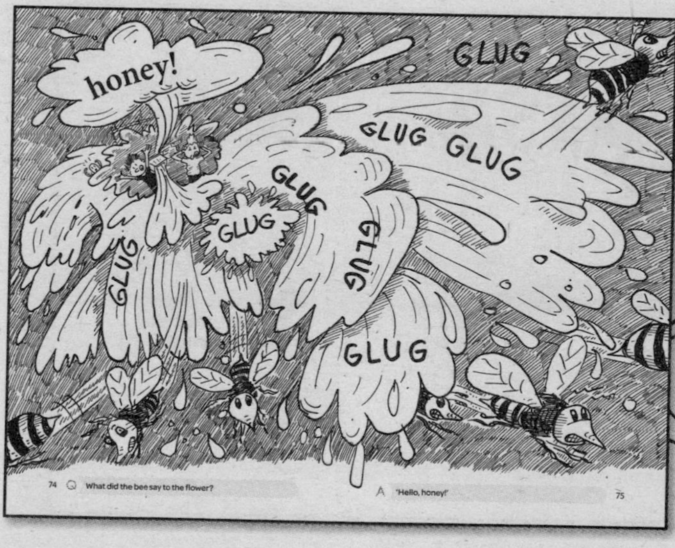

honey!
GLUG
GLUG GLUG
GLUG
GLUG
GLUG
GLUG
GLUG

74 Q What did the bee say to the flower?

A 'Hello, honey!' 75

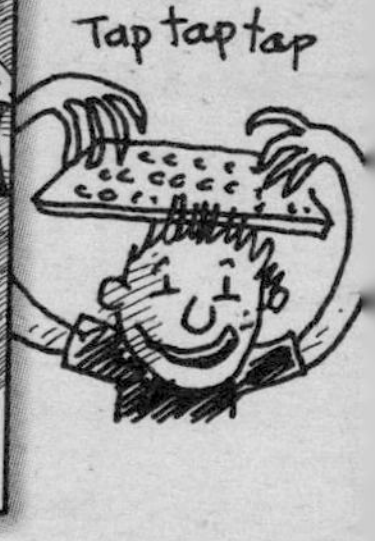

Tap tap tap

and we write …

and we draw…

and we write …

320 Q Why are artists no good in sports matches?

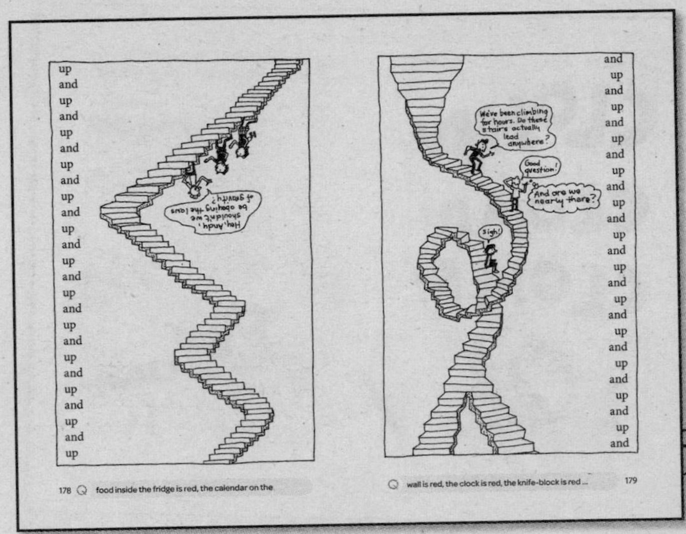
up and up and up and up and up and up and up and up and up and up and up and up and up
Hey, Andy, shouldn't we be obeying the laws of gravity?
We've been climbing for hours. Do these stairs actually lead anywhere?
Good question!
And are we nearly there?
Sigh!
and up and up and up and up and up and up and up and up and up and up and up and up and
178 Q food inside the fridge is red, the calendar on the
Q wall is red, the clock is red, the knife-block is red ...
179

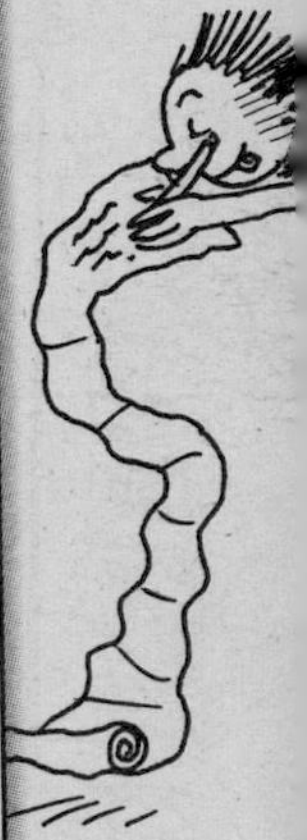

and we write…

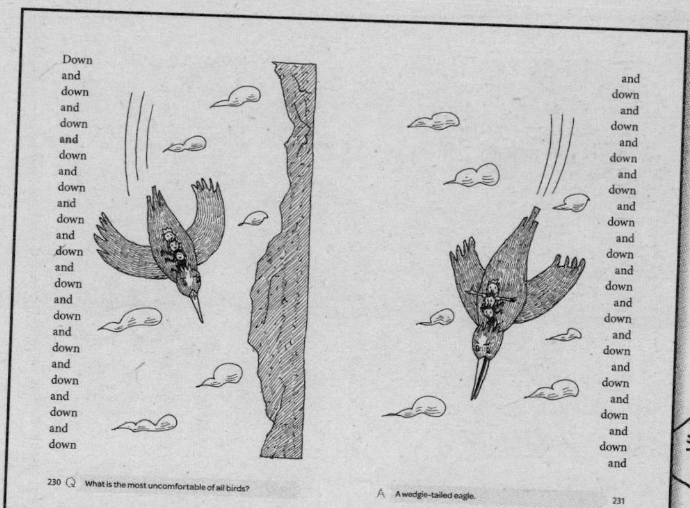
Down and down and down and down and down and down and down and down and down and down and down and down and down
and down and down and down and down and down and down and down and down and down and down and down and
230 Q What is the most uncomfortable of all birds?
A A wedgie-tailed eagle.
231

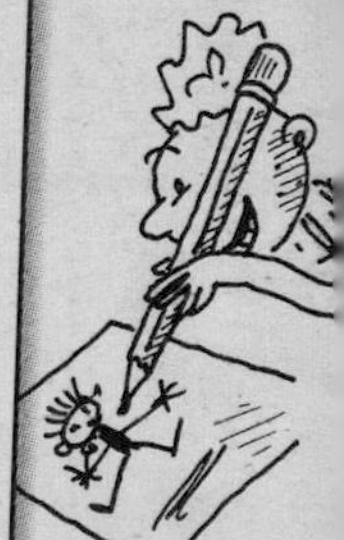

and we draw …

A Because they keep drawing.

and we draw...

and we write ...

Why is a raven like a writing desk?

'But it was only *two* million dollars before,' I say.

'I know,' says Fancy Fish, shrugging, 'but since then the price has gone up.'

'But this is the *Two-Million-Dollar Shop*,' I say.

'Exactly!' he says. 'Nothing *under* two million dollars. That's our promise to you.'

'But you can't just double the price of something for no reason,' says Terry.

'I think you'll find I can,' says Fancy Fish, pointing to a sign above the counter.

288 ◯ What is the easiest way to double your money?

MANAGEMENT RESERVES THE RIGHT TO DOUBLE THE PRICE OF ANY ITEM FOR NO REASON (We apologise for the inconvenience)

A Put it in front of a mirror. 289

and we draw …

Terry laughs so hard he snorts milk out of his nose—and he's not even drinking milk!

'Oh, boy,' says Terry. 'This pencil is amazing!'

'I know,' I say. 'With a pencil *this* funny, we'll be able to write the funniest books ever!'

308 ◯ What do cows give after an earthquake?

'The Joke Writer 2000™ is worth every single dollar we paid for it,' says Terry.

'It sure is,' I say. 'It's worth every bun that knocked us backwards, every flying fridge that almost flattened us, every single stair we climbed on the never-ending staircase and every slimy, revolting, wriggling worm we ate in the worm-snatcher's nest. It's the greatest pencil ever!'

A Milkshakes. 309

and we write …

Until it's all done—even the jokes along the bottom of each page.

CHAPTER 13

THE LAST CHAPTER

'Well, I'm glad *that's* over,' says Terry. 'Now we can all relax. I'm going back to frolic with the lambs in our beautiful sunny meadow.'

A A bluebird.

'And I'm going to keep tracking that high-flying, mountain-dwelling Joke Writer-snatcher,' says Jill. 'They are such fascinating creatures. They're even more rare than high-flying, mountain-dwelling worm-snatchers!'

'Hey, not so fast, you two!' I say. 'Aren't you forgetting something?'

'No, I don't think so,' says Terry.
   'No, I can't think of anything either,' says Jill.

'Okay, then let me ask each of you a riddle,' I say.
   'Oh, goody,' says Terry. 'I love riddles!'

A   Because they can't remember the words.

'All right,' I say. 'Terry's riddle first. What's big and red and gets bigger and redder the angrier it gets and then explodes if a certain writer and illustrator don't get their book delivered by two-thirty today?'

'Hmmm,' says Terry, scratching his chin. 'Beats me.'

'MR BIG NOSE'S NOSE!' I yell.

'Yikes!' says Terry. 'But it's already two twenty-five! How are we going to get our book to him on time?'

'I don't know!' I say. 'But we'd better figure something out … and fast!'

'Hang on,' says Jill. 'What's my riddle? You said you had one for me, too.'

'I sure do,' I say. 'What has 100 heads, 400 legs, lots of fur and is about to go to sleep for six months?'

'Oh, my goodness!' says Jill. 'The answer is *100 bears*! We promised to read them your book before they go to sleep. You have to deliver it to Mr Big Nose or those poor bears will have to go into hibernation without their bear-time story!'

What has 100 heads, 400 legs and is about to go to sleep for six months?

'I know!' I say. 'But how are we going to get our book to Mr Big Nose?'

'We could ask the high-flying, mountain-dwelling worm-snatcher to take us,' says Jill. 'She promised she would help us whenever we were in need, and we are definitely *in need* right now!'

'Let's call her,' I say. 'Everybody ready? On the count of three: one … two … three!'

Q Two silk worms were in a race. Who won?

We've barely had time to close our mouths when the worm-snatcher swoops down, snatches us all up in her mighty talons …

and carries us off to Mr Big Nose's office.

A   It was a tie.

THE DAY THE HIGH-FLYING, MOUNTAIN-DWELLING WORM-SNATCHER SNATCHED US ALL UP AND FLEW US TO MR BIG NOSE'S OFFICE.

Help, Andy!

What can travel around the world while staying in a corner?

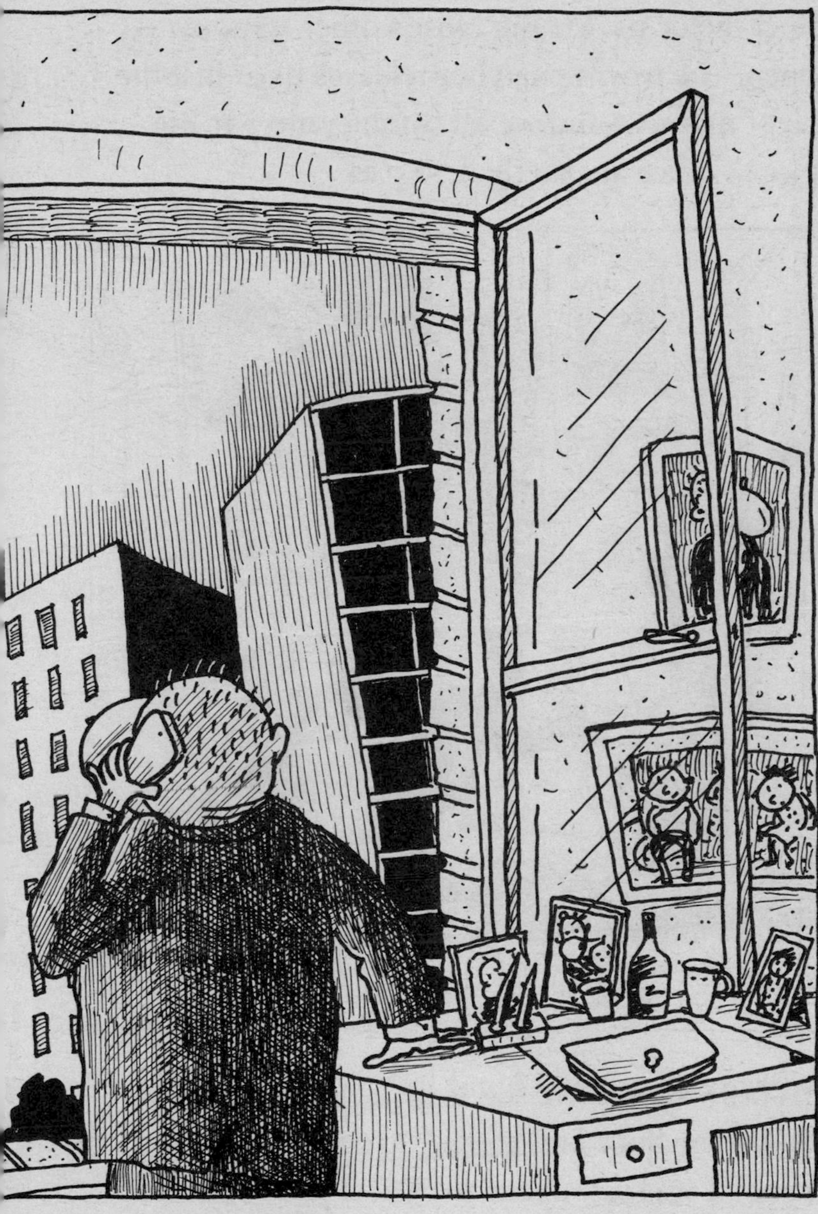

A A stamp.

Luckily for us, Mr Big Nose's office window is open. The worm-snatcher releases us at just the right moment and we all tumble into Mr Big Nose's office at exactly 2.30 p.m.

'At last!' shouts Mr Big Nose as we pick ourselves up off the floor and gather up the pages of our book. 'I was just about to cancel your contract.'

Q What has words but never speaks?

'Sorry, Mr Big Nose,' I say as I hand him the pages. 'But we've been very busy. You can read all about it in *The 104-Storey Treehouse*. Here it is!'

'Is it as good as the last one?' says Mr Big Nose. 'It had better be!'

'Oh, it is,' says Jill. 'It's a great story. Possibly the greatest story ever told.'

A A book.

'Hmmm,' says Mr Big Nose. 'I'll be the judge of that! Well, what are you all standing there for? You can go now. I've got work to do. And so have you—don't forget you have a deadline for next year's book.'

'We won't forget,' I say. 'But before we go, we were wondering if you would be able to do us a very special favour.'

'That depends on what it is,' says Mr Big Nose. 'I'm a very busy man, you know.'

'We know,' I say, 'but would it be possible to put our new book into super-fast production so we can take a copy to read to some bears before they go into hibernation? You see, we promised them we would in exchange for them agreeing to leave the treehouse so we could write the book.'

'Hmmm,' says Mr Big Nose. 'It's highly irregular, but I suppose a promise is a promise—especially where bears are concerned. Wait there and I'll see what I can do.'

THE DAY MR BIG NOSE PUT OUR BOOK INTO SUPER-FAST PRODUCTION

FLING!

① Mr Big Nose sends the pages to the editors.

Odd... strange... Spelling?... plot!? COFFEE

② The editors edit the text and send it to the designer.

③ The designer designs the pages and cover, then converts them to electronic files and sends them to the printer.

④ The printer loads the files into the super fast T4 production machine.

⑤ The pages are printed.

What do snowmen eat for breakfast?

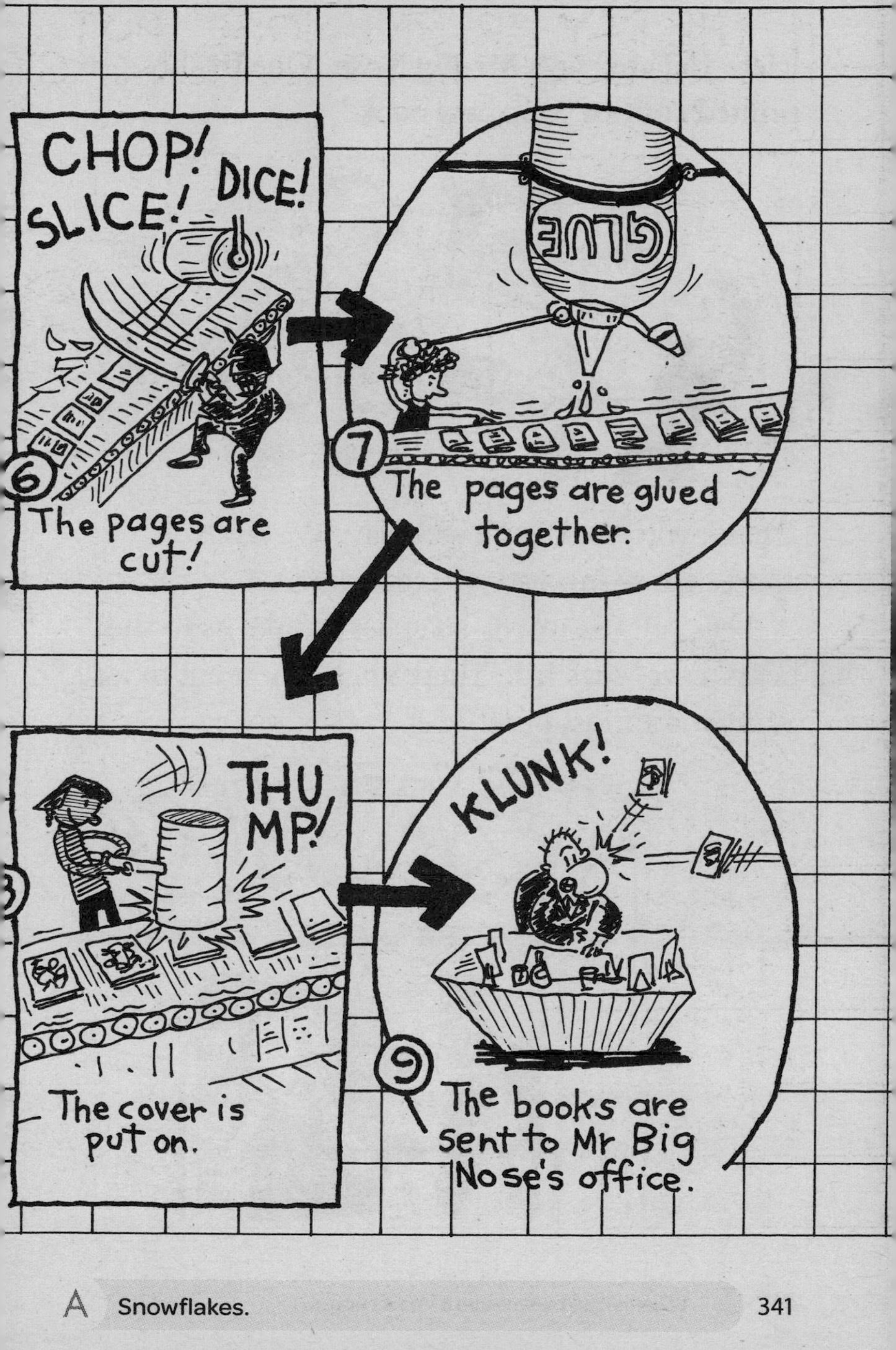
CHOP! SLICE! DICE!
6
The pages are cut!
GLUE
7
The pages are glued together.
THUMP!
8
The cover is put on.
KLUNK!
9
The books are sent to Mr Big Nose's office.

'Here you are,' says Mr Big Nose. 'One freshly printed copy of your new book.'

'Thank you, Mr Big Nose,' I say. 'We really appreciate it—and so will the bears.'

'Let's call the worm-snatcher to take us to the bears' cave,' says Jill. 'There's not a moment to lose. Winter is almost here!'

Once again the worm-snatcher appears and snatches us all up, along with our new book.

A Run faster than everyone else.

THE DAY THE HIGH-FLYING, SNATCHER SNATCHED US UP AND FLEW US TO THE BEARS'

MOUNTAIN-DWELLING WORM—
FROM MR BIG NOSE'S OFFICE
CAVE.

A   Nothing, just run.   345

When we arrive the bears are all in their pyjamas, sitting up in a 100-bear bed.

What did the blanket say to the mattress?

They let out a huge 100-bear roar.

'That means, "Hooray for Andy, Terry and Jill!"'
says Jill.

Terry, Jill and I sit down in a big chair, get cosy and start reading to the bears.

Q   What's the last thing you take off before bed?

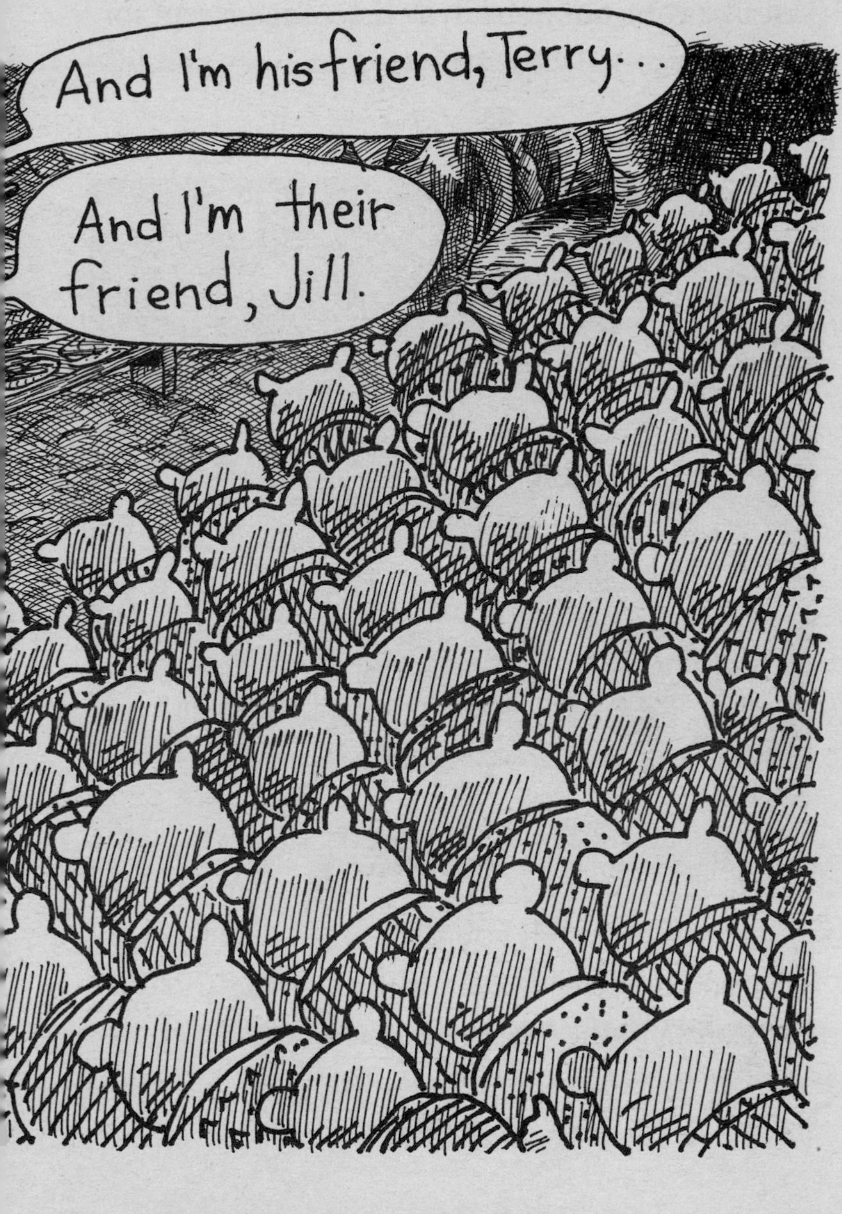
And I'm his friend, Terry...
And I'm their friend, Jill.

A few hours later I finally reach this, the last page (just like you), but nobody is listening (except for you, of course). All the bears—and Terry and Jill—are fast asleep.

I've got to admit I'm feeling pretty sleepy myself. I might just nap for a little while—well, probably most of winter to tell you the truth—and then Terry and I will get busy adding another thirteen new storeys to the treehouse. Goodnight!

THE END

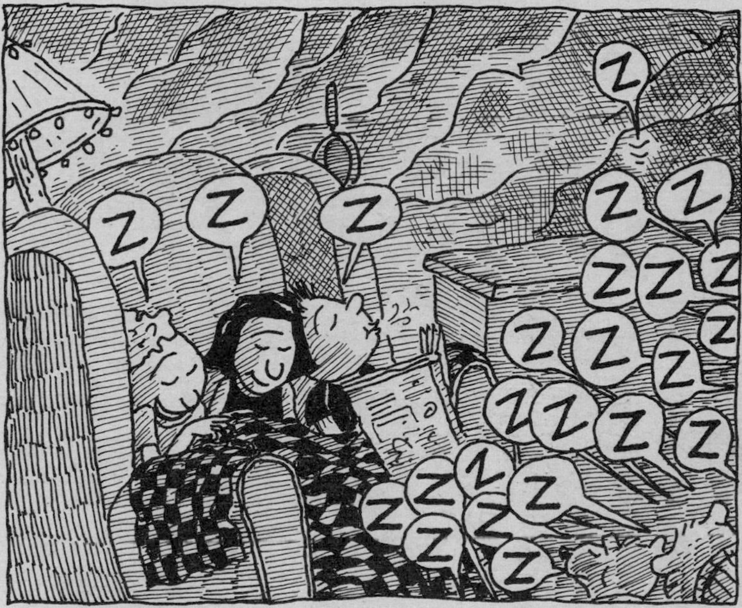
Z
Z
Z
Z
Z
Z
Z
Z
Z
Z
Z
Z
Z
Z
Z
Z
Z
Z
Z
Z
Z
Z
Z
Z
Z

A A library.

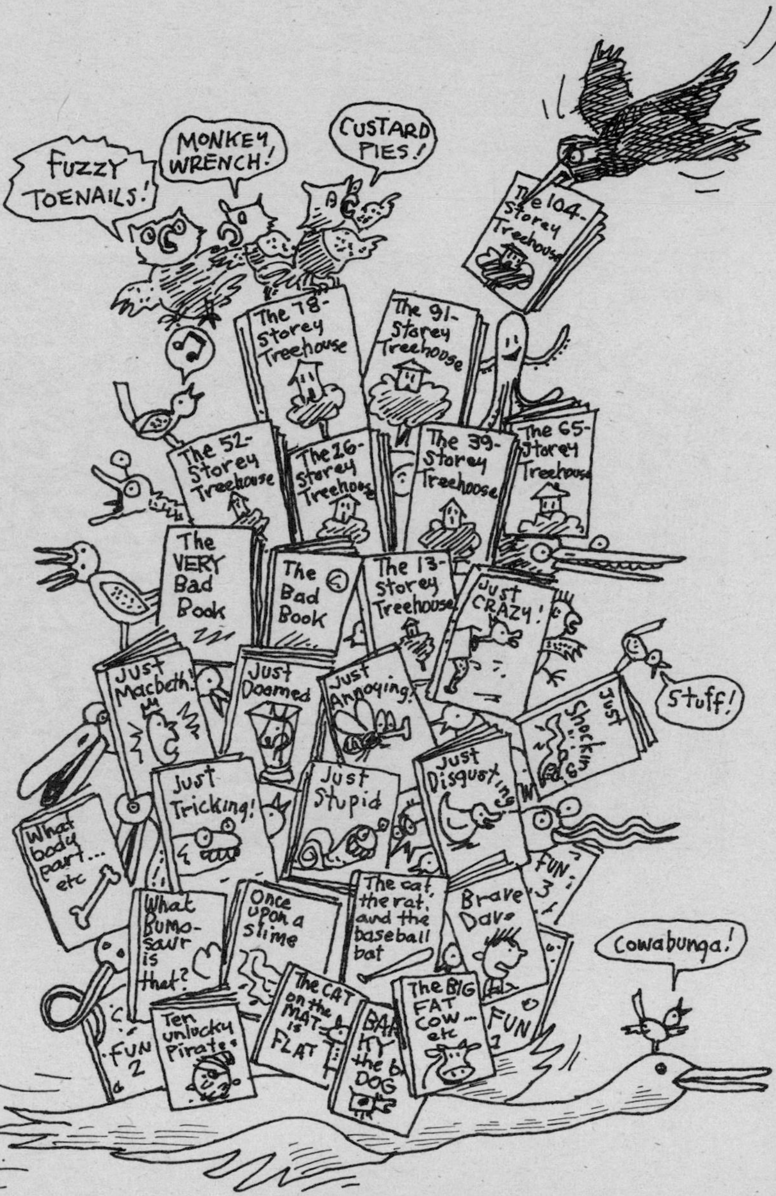

FUZZY TOENAILS!
MONKEY WRENCH!
CUSTARD PIES!
The 104-Storey Treehouse
The 78-Storey Treehouse
The 91-Storey Treehouse
The 52-Storey Treehouse
The 26-Storey Treehouse
The 39-Storey Treehouse
The 65-Storey Treehouse
The VERY Bad Book
The Bad Book
The 13-Storey Treehouse
Just CRAZY!
Just Macbeth!
Just Doomed
Just Annoying!
Just Shockin
Stuff!
Just Tricking!
Just Stupid
Just Disgusting
What body part... etc
FUN 3
What Bumosaur is that?
Once upon a slime
The cat, the rat, and the baseball bat
Brave Dave
Cowabunga!
Ten unlucky Pirates
The CAT on the MAT is FLAT
BARKY the b DOG
The BIG FAT COW... etc
FUN 1
FUN 2

The 117-Storey Treehouse

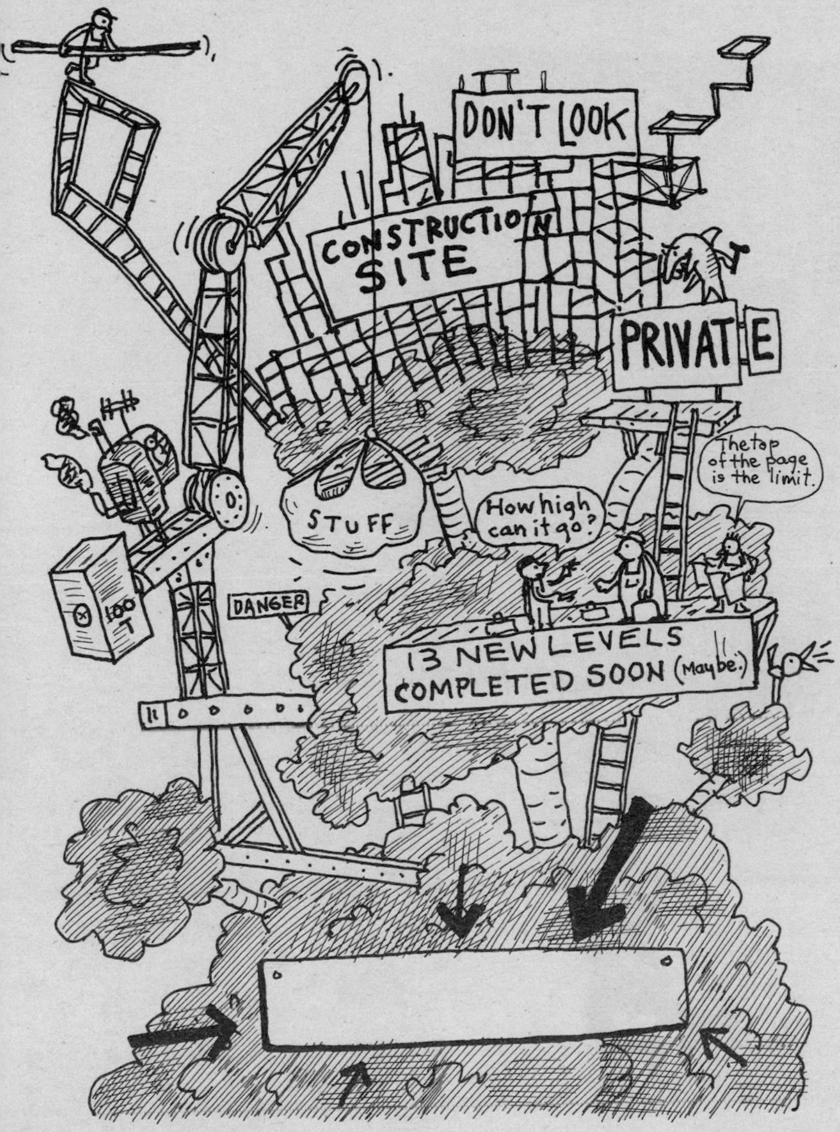
DON'T LOOK
CONSTRUCTION SITE
PRIVATE
The top of the page is the limit.
How high can it go?
STUFF
DANGER
100 T
13 NEW LEVELS COMPLETED SOON (Maybe.)

Lots of laughs

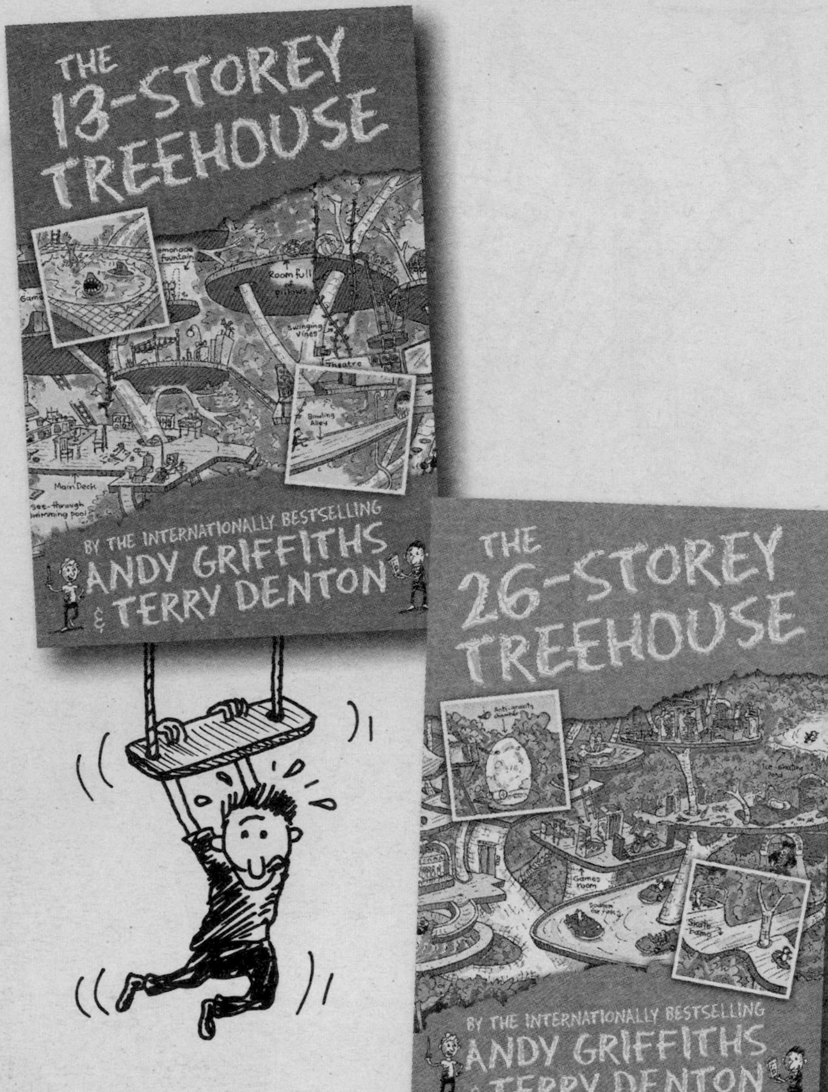
THE 13-STOREY TREEHOUSE
BY THE INTERNATIONALLY BESTSELLING
ANDY GRIFFITHS
& TERRY DENTON
THE 26-STOREY TREEHOUSE
BY THE INTERNATIONALLY BESTSELLING
ANDY GRIFFITHS
& TERRY DENTON

at every level!

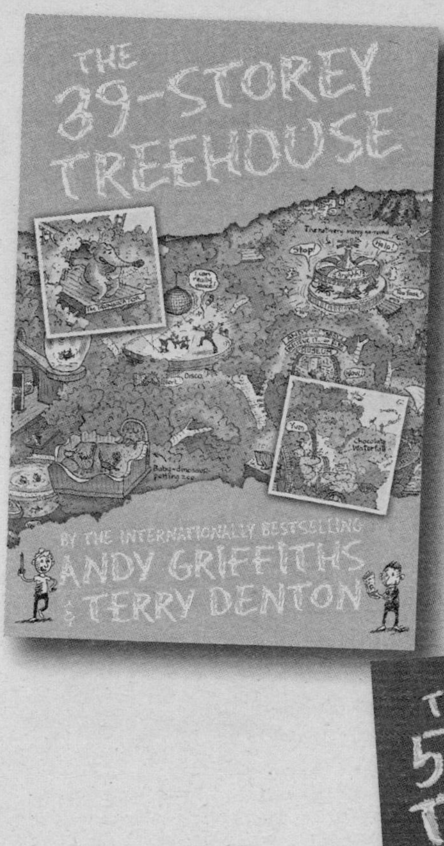
THE
39-STOREY
TREEHOUSE
BY THE INTERNATIONALLY BESTSELLING
ANDY GRIFFITHS
& TERRY DENTON

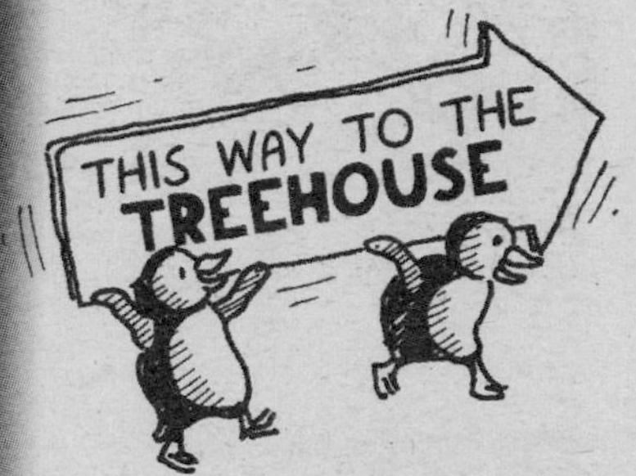
THIS WAY TO THE
TREEHOUSE

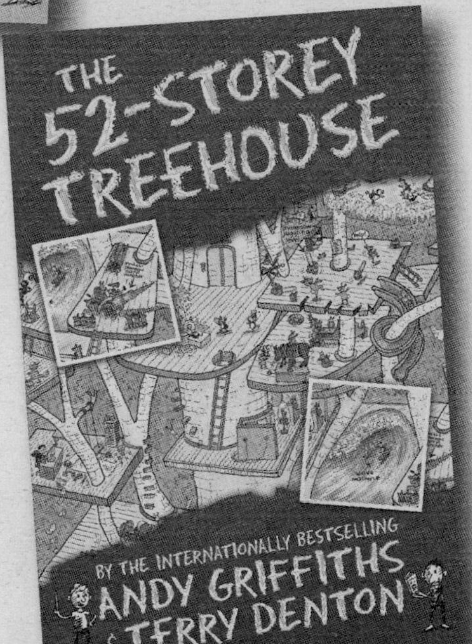
THE
52-STOREY
TREEHOUSE
BY THE INTERNATIONALLY BESTSELLING
ANDY GRIFFITHS
& TERRY DENTON

Lots of laughs

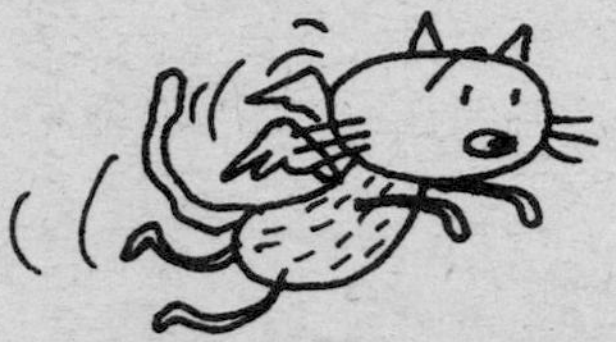

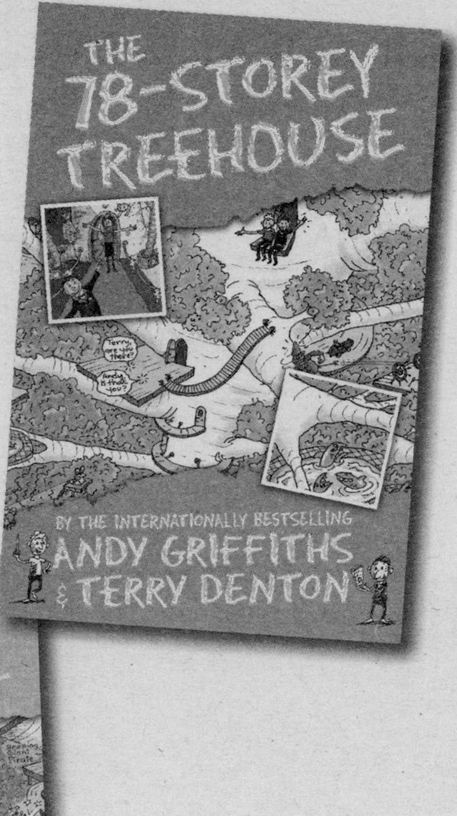
THE 78-STOREY TREEHOUSE
BY THE INTERNATIONALLY BESTSELLING
ANDY GRIFFITHS
& TERRY DENTON

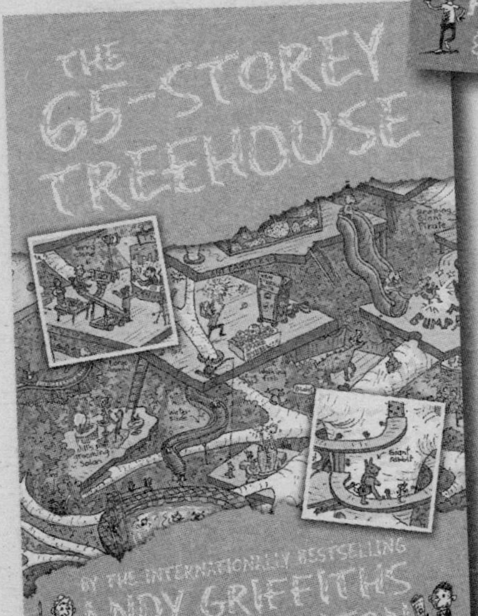
THE 65-STOREY TREEHOUSE
BY THE INTERNATIONALLY BESTSELLING
ANDY GRIFFITHS
& TERRY DENTON

at every level!

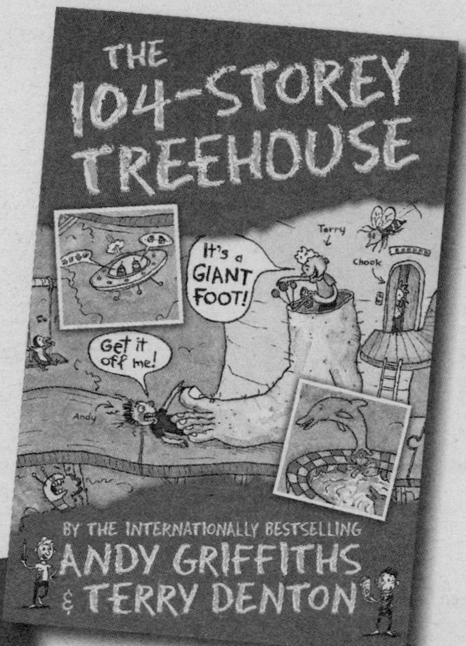
THE 104-STOREY TREEHOUSE
Terry
Chook
It's a GIANT FOOT!
Get it off me!
Andy
BY THE INTERNATIONALLY BESTSELLING
ANDY GRIFFITHS & TERRY DENTON

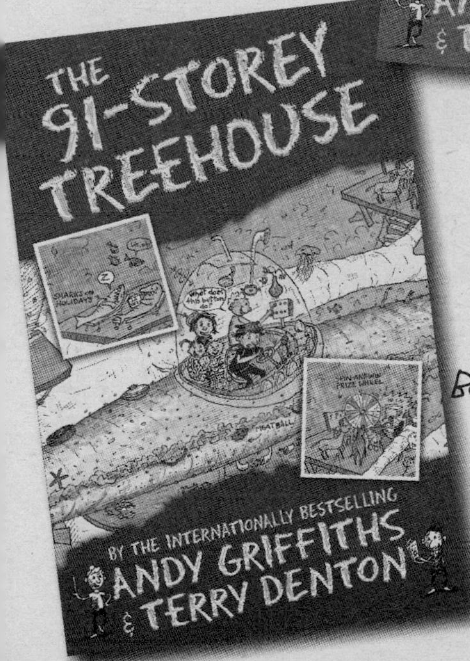
THE 91-STOREY TREEHOUSE
BY THE INTERNATIONALLY BESTSELLING
ANDY GRIFFITHS & TERRY DENTON

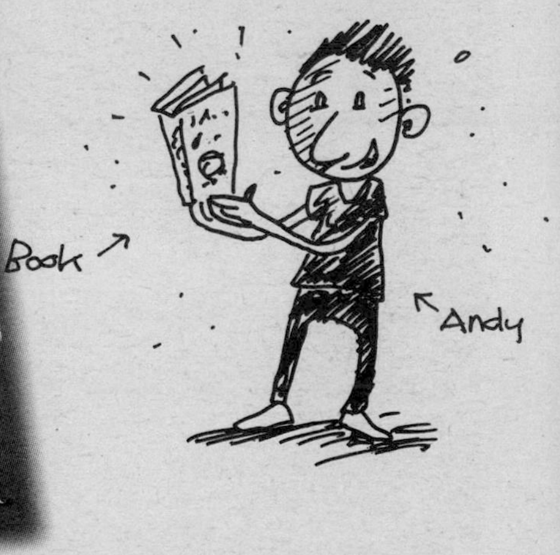
Book
Andy

Lots of laughs at every level!

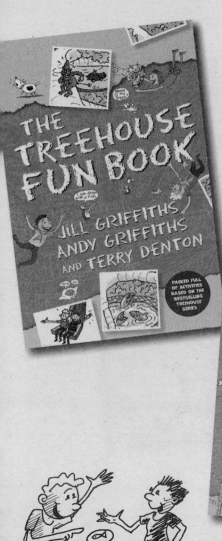

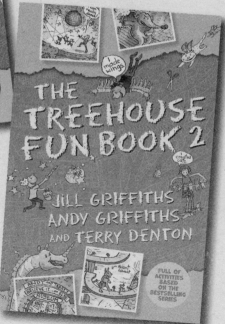

FULL OF ACTIVITIES BASED ON THE BESTSELLING SERIES

Coming soon!

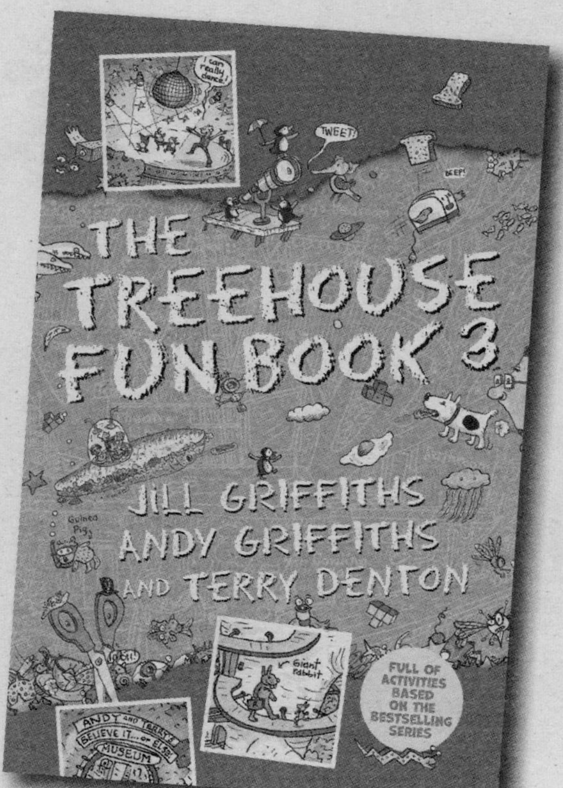

THE TREEHOUSE FUN BOOK 3
JILL GRIFFITHS
ANDY GRIFFITHS
AND TERRY DENTON
FULL OF ACTIVITIES BASED ON THE BESTSELLING SERIES
I can really dance!
TWEET!
Guinea Pig
Giant rabbit
ANDY AND TERRY'S BELIEVE IT... OR ELSE! MUSEUM